William's Crowded Hours

Also available in Armada

Just—William
William—The Bad
William—The Bold
William's Happy Days
William—The Detective
Still—William
William and the Pop Singers
William and the Moon Rocket

First published in this abridged edition in 1967 by
George Newnes Ltd., London.

This edition was first published in 1972 by
William Collins Sons & Co. Ltd., 14 St. James's Place,
London SW1A 1PF

Printed in Great Britain by
Love & Malcomson Ltd., Brighton Road,
Redhill, Surrey.

William's
Crowded Hours

Richmal Crompton

Illustrated by Thomas Henry

CONTENTS

CHAPTER I

WILLIAM AND THE TEMPORARY HISTORY MASTER

WILLIAM had thought that school could not possibly be worse than it was, but quite suddenly—half-way through the term—he discovered his mistake. The history master, a mild and elderly man, conveniently short-sighted, conveniently deaf, and still more conveniently fond of expounding his own historical theories without in the least minding whether anyone listened to them or not, caught scarlet fever and was removed to hospital.

For a few glorious lessons William's form spent the history hour officially doing homework, but in reality indulging in such sports and pastimes as dart-throwing, earwig racing, ruler-and-rubber cricket, and ink slinging. Then the "temporary" arrived—a small, smug man with protruding teeth and a manner that hovered between the hearty, the jocular, and the sarcastic. He had, moreover, modern theories about the teaching of history. He believed it making it real by acting it. When he gave a lesson on the Magna Charta one of the boys had to be King John and the others the turbulent barons. When he gave a lesson on Charles I, one of them had to be Charles I, and another the executioner, and so on. The novelty of this proceeding had long worn off as far as Mr. Renies himself was concerned, and he now relieved the monotony of it as far as possible by choosing for the principal and most dramatic parts boys who were obviously devoid of histrionic talent. This enabled him to make clever little jibes at their clumsiness, jibes that were always rewarded by the sycophantic titters of the other boys. Mr. Renies loved these sycophantic titters. He didn't consider them sycophantic, of course. He considered them honest tributes to his sparkling wit and brilliant flashes of humour. Mr. Renies, it is perhaps unnecessary to add, thought a great deal of himself, more in fact than most other people thought of him. He was certainly clever in picking out the right boy for his butt—self-conscious, inarticulate, and yet not insensitive.

On the first day on which Mr. Renies faced William's form he looked round for his butt and his eye fell on William. William, it must be admitted, looked the part to perfection.

"What's your name?" said Mr. Renies.

"Brown," admitted William suspiciously.

Mr. Renies' face beamed with anticipatory pleasure.

"Well, Brown," he said kindly, "suppose you come out here and give us your idea of Charles the First before the House of Commons demanding the arrest of the five members . . ."

Alone or with his Outlaws William could act the hero in the most stirring scenes that the imagination could possibly conceive, but to be ordered to act as part of a lesson by this objectionable little man was quite another thing. Reluctantly he came up to the front of the class. There he stood, purple-faced with anger and embarrassment, glaring ferociously at Mr. Renies and the class. Mr. Renies' smile broadened. He enlivened the lesson with frequent references to "this kingly figure" . . . "this mien of majesty," and was rewarded as usual by a chorus of titters from boys who were relieved that his choice had fallen on William and not on them.

The next day he ordered William to impersonate Prince Rupert and the day after that Oliver Cromwell. William impersonated both by the simple means of staring furiously and doggedly in front of him, and Mr. Renies' enjoyment increased.

He referred to him as "this noble youth," "this

6

Reluctantly William came up to the front of the class.
There he stood, purple with anger and embarrassment,
glaring ferociously at the master.

valiant hero," and even as "this spirited young
actor."

William disliked it, but saw no other course than to
endure it. He had no weapon against Mr. Renies
except in his imagination, and he worked his imagination very hard during those days. There had been a
side show in the last fair that had visited the village
called "Picture of 200 different forms of Torture," and
William had paid his 1*d.* entrance fee and spent an
enthralled half-hour in the tent. He now put Mr.
Renies in imagination through every one of the two
hundred forms of torture. As Mr. Renies, gay and
debonair, stood at his desk and poured forth his
stream of little witticisms, he had no idea of course

7

that William saw him writhing on a rack or struggling in boiling oil. In fact so horrible and so real were these pictures to William that he couldn't help feeling that he had scored. After all, what was being made to feel a fool before the class in comparison with being impaled on spikes and rolled down-hill in a barrel full of nails—things that happened to Mr. Renies several times an hour? But even Mr. Renies could go too far.

"Now, Brown," he said, with his toothy smile, "we must think out a nice part for you for next revision lesson. How about—he rose to dazzling heights of wit—making you Henrietta Maria and I'll be Buckingham and come to woo you? That would be nice, boys, wouldn't it?" The bored titter that Mr. Renies looked upon as a spontaneous tribute to his wit broke out again dutifully, and Mr. Renies continued: "Our young actor doesn't look pleased. . . . You must come round to my house some evening, my friend, and we'll practise some of these rôles together."

William began to be dimly aware that this state of things could not go on, and that something must be done about it, but it was a quite justifiable action on the part of Mr. Renies that finally roused him.

Mr. Renies was in the habit of confiscating any article with which he saw his pupils playing, and, finding William opening the back of his watch and trying to replace a little wheel that he had taken out to sharpen a pencil point, he confiscated it. The watch had not been going for some weeks, and in any case William never cared what time it was, so it cannot he said that the loss of the watch as a means of telling the time seriously inconvenienced him. In fact, if his mother had not had a letter from the aunt who had given him the watch, saying that she was coming to see them the next week and adding facetiously that she need not bring her grandfather clock because William would be able to tell her the time by his nice new watch, William would never have thought of it again.

The fact that the watch wasn't going wouldn't matter, of course. His aunt, aware that it was a cheap watch and unaware that William took from it regularly any of its component parts that he needed for his various experiments (such as making a motor-launch, or a treadwheel for his pet stag beetle), would merely have offered to pay for it being mended, as she had already done once or twice. But the fact that it had passed out of his possession entirely would matter a great deal. Aunts are notoriously touchy on such points, and it would probably matter so much that she would not give him the customary tip on her departure. Therefore William decided by hook or by crook to recover his watch. He gave Mr. Renies the chance of acting magnanimously by asking for it. He asked for it when Mr. Renies was alone in the form-room, and, as there was no appreciative audience to render him its homage of titters, Mr. Renies wasted none of his famous wit on William, but merely snapped "Certainly not!"

Therefore no course was left to William, as William saw the situation, but that of entering Mr. Renies' house, where presumably Mr. Renies kept his ill-gotten gains, and taking the watch from Mr. Renies as lawlessly as, William considered, Mr. Renies had taken it from him.

And so the night before his aunt's visit William approached the history master's house (where Mr. Renies was temporarily domiciled), having left Mr. Renies in his form-room correcting exercises.

He knocked boldly at the front door. A maid wearing a grimy apron and a dreamy expression came to answer his knock.

"I've called with a message from Mr. Renies," said William, meeting her eye squarely, "he says you needn't stop in any longer this evening. You can go out now."

The maid, fortunately for William, was of a simple and credulous disposition. Moreover she was in love. To go out meant meeting the beloved, therefore she was willing to believe implicitly any message that told her to go out.

"What about his supper?" she said.

"Oh, he won't be a minute," said William reassuringly. "He says just leave it ready."

"What about locking up?" said the maid, who was already in imagination walking down a country lane clasped tightly in the stalwart arm of the beloved.

"He says put the key on the window-sill," said William.

A few minutes later the maid laid the key upon the window-sill and flew on winged feet to Paradise and the beloved.

A few minutes later still William took the key from the window-sill and opened the front door.

*   *   *   *   *

Mr. Renies walked slowly up to his house. He felt pleased with the world in general and himself in particular. He had finished his corrections early, he had got some good fun out of that kid—what was his name—Brown—he was going home to a delicious supper of pheasant, bread sauce, baked potatoes, brussels sprouts, followed by a pineapple cream and a savoury. Mr. Renies liked to do himself well, but it wasn't often that he could rise to such heights as this. The supper was in honour of the pheasant that had been sent to him by a cousin who was staying at a "shoot." Mr. Renies had been looking forward to it all day.

He opened his front door and stood for a minute in the hall, dilating his nostrils and drawing in the delicious odour with an anticipatory smile. Then he hung up his hat, washed his hands, called out: "I'm ready, Ellen," and went toward the dining-room, rubbing his hands, and smacking his lips. He flung open the door and entered. And there the

10

first shock awaited him. Upon the table stood a dish containing the well-picked carcase of a pheasant, flanked by empty vegetable dishes. At his place was an empty well-scraped plate that had recently contained pheasant, bread sauce, baked potatoes, gravy and brussels sprouts. On it were laid at an unconventional angle the knife and fork that had evidently been used in the consumption of the repast. There was an empty dish that had evidently once contained a pineapple cream and another dish that had evidently contained a savoury. For a moment Mr. Renies was literally paralysed with horror and amazement. His eyes grew fixed and glassy. His mouth dropped open. Then he cried: "Ellen!" and rushed to the kitchen. The kitchen was empty. Ellen's cap and apron were hung neatly behind the door. He called: "Ellen!" still more wildly, but no one answered. It was quite clear that Ellen was no longer in the house. Mr. Renies dashed upstairs to his study. And there the second shock awaited him. The drawer in which he kept the articles that he confiscated in school was open and empty.

"Burglars!" was his first thought but he found on examination that nothing else in the room was missing. Then he heard a sound in the big cupboard by the window, and for a moment the wild idea flashed into his head that rats were responsible for everything—the eating of his supper, the emptying of the drawers and the strange noise in the cupboard. He remembered in time, however, that rats do not use knives and forks. He flung open the cupboard door and there he got his third shock. For William crouched in the cupboard blinking at him.

William had not really meant to eat Mr. Renies' supper. He had peeped into the dining-room and found the meal laid there. It looked very appetising, and William was very hungry. William decided to eat a very little of it, so little that Mr. Renies couldn't possibly notice. It wasn't till he discovered

11

that he had eaten so much that Mr. Renies couldn't possibly help noticing it, that he decided that he might as well finish it. So he finished it and thoroughly enjoyed it. It was, he decided, the best meal he'd ever had in his life (better even than Christmas dinner because there was no one there to worry him about manners), and worth any consequences. Then he went upstairs to find his watch. He found it quite easily in the first drawer he opened. With it were a penknife of Ginger's, a mouth organ of Douglas's, a catapult of Henry's and numerous other articles belonging to other boys. William decided that he might as well take them all. He would give their property back to Ginger and Henry and Douglas and sell the rest to their owners. William possessed a strong commercial instinct. Just as he was putting the last article (a pistol belonging to Smith minimus) into his pocket he heard someone enter the house. He stood still and listened. Soon there came a ferocious bellow, angry cries of "Ellen!" and the sound of heavy footsteps ascending the stairs. Without a moment's hesitation William flung himself into the only cupboard the room possessed and closed the doors. Unfortunately the cupboard was already full of other things than William, and William's figure, though small, was not the sort of figure to accommodate itself to the thin zig-zag line of space left between a pile of books, a duplicating machine, half a dozen croquet mallets, a dozen Indian clubs, an old-fashioned camera on a stand and a large moth-eaten stag's head with branching antlers. With great difficulty he took up a posture that was in the shape of the letter S, but one of the stag's antlers was digging so mercilessly into his neck that he moved slightly in order to relieve the pressure, and knocked over the pile of books. Almost immediately the cupboard door was flung open, and the amazed and furious face of Mr. Renies appeared. William was glad to be saved from the murderous attack of the moth-eaten stag, but otherwise he realised that the situation was a delicate one. There was no doubt at all that Mr. Renies was very angry. He dragged William out by his ear and thundered:

"What is the meaning of this?"

For a moment William was at a loss how to answer, then inspiration came to him. He assumed a vacant expression.

"Please, sir," he said, "you asked me to come to your house an' practise actin' history scenes some evening, so I came, an' I was jus' practis'n' bein' Charles the First in hidin' when you came in."

Mr. Renies sputtered angrily. His eyes fell upon the empty drawer.

"And did you *dare*," he stormed, "to open a private drawer of mine and empty it?"

Inspiration again came to William. He realised with surprise that he knew more history than he had thought.

"No, sir," he said innocently, "I was practisin' being Jack Cade's rebellion lootin' and plunderin'."

Then the memory of the supreme outrage of that evening came back to Mr. Renies, and for a minute his fury and anguish deprived him of the power of speech. Finally he stuttered:

"And—and—and—downstairs—was it *you* who *dared* to——"

William by now had his wits well about him.

"That?" he said. "Oh yes, sir. I was practisin' actin' that king that died of a surfeit of lampreys. I couldn't find any lampreys so I jus' had to eat what I could find. I didn't die of it either but that wasn't my fault."

With a howl of fury Mr. Renies flung himself upon William, but William was already half-way downstairs.

"I'm practisin' bein' Charles II fleein' after the battle of Worcester," he called over his shoulder as he ran.

Mr. Renies plunged downstairs after him. This was

an occasion for immediate revenge. A man as deeply outraged in his dignity and his stomach as Mr. Renies had been does not defer punishment till the next morning. The pleasant perfume of roast pheasant that hung about the hall increased his anger to the point of madness as he passed through it. In the dusk he could see the figure of William fleeing down the road. He followed, and fury lent wings to him. Fury, in fact, lent such wings that William began to feel slightly disconcerted. It is not easy to run really fast on such a meal as William had just partaken of, and there was no doubt that Mr. Renies was gaining on him. That retribution must follow the evening's exploit sooner or later William was well aware, but he preferred it to be later rather than sooner. Certainly he didn't want to receive it at the hands of an enraged Mr. Renies in the middle of the road. Mr. Renies was a better runner than he looked, and slowly but steadily he was gaining on his quarry. It was too late now even to plunge through the hedge into a field. The time it would take to turn off from the road would deliver him into his enemy's hands. And William rightly judged that it would take more than a hedge to stop the raging pheasantless man behind him. He was quite near him now. Almost upon him. Only a miracle could save William. Turning a sharp bend in the road he ran into his sister, who was taking a leisurely walk with a girl friend. Nimbly William dodged aside and took cover behind them. Round the corner immediately after him came Mr. Renies, his arms outstretched to catch that little fiend who was at last within his grasp. He collided violently with Ethel and her friend. He lost his balance and clung to them to save himself—an arm round the neck of each. From behind them came William's voice breathless but quite distinct.

"This is Mr. Renies, Ethel," he said. "He's our history master. He goes about actin' history scenes. He's actin' " . . . the sight of Mr. Renies, still clasping the necks of Ethel and her friend in an attempt to recover his balance suggested, an irresistible parallel—"he's actin' he's Henry the Eighth now," he ended and disappeared into the dusk.

He didn't disappear alone, however. Mr. Renies, his fury again roused to boiling-point, dashed after him. William had had a slight start, but the added fury of Mr. Renies' spirit again seemed to give speed to his feet. Again he was on the point of catching William, when William suddenly darted through the open garden gate belonging to a house that bordered the road. William knew the garden well. There was a lily pond in the middle of the lawn. William sometimes took a forbidden short cut through the garden and took the lily pond literally in his stride. He cleared it now with a skill born of long practise. Mr. Renies was at a disadvantage. He didn't know that there was a lily pond and in the dusk he did not notice it. He fol'owed William's flying figure and—found himself up to the shoulders in water. The sound of the splash and of the shout of anger and surprise that accompanied it, brought an elderly lady down from the house to investigate. She found a man floundering in her lily pond and a boy standing by the side watching him.

"What on earth does this mean?" asked the lady majestically.

Mr. Renies tried to explain, but he couldn't, because he'd swallowed a pint of water and several lily buds in his sudden descent.

"Is he drunk?" went on the lady.

"No," said William, "he's not exactly drunk. He's Mr. Renies, our history master. He goes about acting history scenes. He's acting now that this is the sea, that he's the king's son that was drowned in the sea and never smiled again."

"He must be *mad*," said the lady indignantly.

Mr. Renies again made frenzied efforts to explain, but all he could do was to spit out lily buds.

"He's not exactly mad," said William indulgently, "He's just got this craze for actin' history scenes. I

15

go about with him to see he doesn't do too much damage."

"But he's *ruining* the lily pond," said the lady.

"I know," said William sadly, "but he *would* go into it. When he thinks of a scene he wants to act nothin' can stop him."

The lady turned to Mr. Renies indignantly.

"You ought to be ashamed of yourself," she said, "get out of my pond at once or I'll send for the police."

William had discreetly vanished into the dusk.

"Listen!" sputtered Mr. Renies wildly, but the lady had turned on her heel and gone into the house, whither she sent a man servant to expel Mr. Renies from the pond and to inform him that if he wasn't out of the garden within five minutes she was going to send for the police.

Dripping and dishevelled, Mr. Renies stumbled out of the garden gate into the road. He peered about him, but there was no sign of William. Then from above his head came a small distinct voice.

"I'm actin' being Charles II in the oak tree now . . ."

Mr. Renies ignored it. Wet, cold and hungry he staggered homewards.

* * * * *

Mr. Renies' first thought was to lay the whole matter before the headmaster. For a boy to go to a master's house, eat his supper, ransack his drawers, hide in his cupboard, then lead him a dance over the countryside, was surely a crime unknown before in the annals of school life. Then Mr. Renies began to wonder whether it would be really wise to lay the whole matter before the headmaster. The episodes that took place in his house were all right. It was the episodes that took place outside his house that made him hesitate. He saw himself clinging to those two girls, he saw himself floundering in the lily pond. . . . Of course, he needn't mention those episodes, but he was beginning to know William a little better, and he was afraid that William's conscience would lead him to "confess" them. He saw himself the laughing-stock of the village. As things were, that might be avoided. He had heard one of the two girls say crossly: "That *awful* boy." Obviously they knew William and felt only annoyance with him. He could go to see the lady of the lily pond, and make up some story that would satisfy her. (He could say that he thought the boy had fallen into the lily pond and had plunged in to rescue him.) There wasn't any reason why anyone else should know anything about it. William might tell? Mr. Renies had a shrewd idea that, properly treated, William would not tell. . . .

He changed from his wet clothes and sat down to write to his cousin thanking him for the pheasant. He said with bitterness in his heart that it had been delicious. A funny thing about that boy, he reflected as he stamped and addressed the letter. He'd thought him a perfectly safe butt for his little jokes. One did sometimes make mistakes however. . . .

The next morning Mr. Renies entered the classroom, sat down at the master's desk, and said: "Open your note-books, please."

"Please, sir, aren't we going to have any acting today?" said a boy in the front row.

"Acting?" repeated Mr. Renies, as if he did not understand.

"Yes, sir. Acting history scenes."

"Acting history scenes?" said Mr. Renies in a tone of great surprise and indignation, "of course not. I never heard of such a thing. Open your note-books and take down the following dates." Then politely, almost affectionately, in the tone in which a master speaks to a favourite pupil, he added: "Would you mind cleaning the board for me, please, Brown?"

A close observer would have noticed a rather peculiar smile on William's face, as he rose obediently from his desk and began to clean the board.

CHAPTER II

A CROWDED HOUR WITH WILLIAM

WILLIAM'S mother was making cakes at the kitchen table, and William was watching the operation with melancholy interest.

"I can't think what you *do* it for," he said.

"Do what for, dear?" she asked absently.

"Cook it," said William, "it's much nicer before you start cooking it," and added bitterly, "not that I've ever had enough to taste hardly."

"But you always scrape out the dish, dear," protested his mother. "I'm going to let you scrape out the dish now. And the spoon."

William laughed sardonically.

"Huh! An' there's likely to be a lot on, isn't there?" he said. "Anyone'd think you were tryin' to *starve* me the way you scrape it out."

"But you've had a very good breakfast," his mother reminded him.

"Breakfast!" ejaculated William with infinite contempt.

She began to scrape out the cake mixture and put it into little tins. William watched her with agonised eyes and ejaculations of incredulous surprise.

"Gosh! Fancy scrapin' it out like *that*! Crumbs! You'll have the basin in *bits* soon, scrapin' it like that. It must be a jolly strong basin. Why, you've not left enough to *see*. A *fly* wouldn't bother to eat what you've left. A——"

"Now, William," his mother interrupted him firmly,

"I've left quite a lot. If you don't want it, of course, you needn't have it. I'll put the basin to soak in the sink."

But William, who had been talking for talking's sake and because he considered that to admit that a reasonable amount of cake mixture had been left in the dish might prejudice his chance of getting more next time, hastily seized it and set to work upon it earnestly.

"It's jolly good," he said as he emerged from the final stage of the ceremony that left the dish as clean as if it had been washed.

"Oh *William*," sighed his mother, "you've got it on your hair *and* your ears."

"Where?" said William as if interested to hear that traces of the delicious mixture was still in existence.

"Go and wash, William," commanded his mother sternly.

William went to wash and returned to find his mother closing the oven door, having deposited the tray of cakes inside.

"Jus' let me eat *one* of 'em raw," he said, "then I promise I won't eat any of the others cooked. I'd rather have one raw than hundreds cooked."

"No, William," said his mother, "they're not for you in any case. They're for the Women's Guild Exhibition."

"The Women's Guild?" repeated William in indignant horror. "What're *they* wantin' our cakes for?"

"It's a competition for home-made things," explained Mrs. Brown patiently, "and I'm entering for the cakes. There's cakes and jam and bottled fruits and wine and pickles and things like that."

"What do you get for a prize?" said William.

"A badge."

"A *what*?"

"A badge."

"*Crumbs!*" said William. "Nothin' more than that?"

"No. It's the honour and glory that counts."

"I'd rather have cakes than honour and glory any day," said William simply. "What happens to the cakes?"

"They go to the Cottage Hospital for the sick people."

"Gosh!" said William. "Cakes like that *wasted* on sick people! Well, I've been sick, so I *know*. I think it's *unkind* to send 'em to sick people. Tell you what——"

But William's mother cut him short.

"Now, William, don't stay in here chattering. I'm busy. You can help me carry the cakes down to the Village Hall after tea if you like."

William greeted this suggestion with an ironic laugh.

"Huh! Thanks. It's *jolly* kind of you to let me carry down cakes that I'm not allowed to eat and that are going to be used makin' sick people worse. *Jolly* kind!"

But still William never liked to be out of anything that was going on, and after tea he appeared as if by accident as his mother was just setting off with her basket.

"I jus' happen to be goin' down to the village," he said casually, "so I'll come along with you."

She refused his offer to carry the basket and they set off together to the Village Hall.

There William watched the scene with amazed interest. Crowds of women were placing dishes of cakes, jars of jam or pickles, on long trestle tables, behind which stood other women wearing blue overalls and expressions that became more and more apprehensive as they surveyed the growing array of products that would have to be judged.

"My dear," murmured one to the other. "I had indigestion for *months* after it last year, and there seems to be even more this."

William overheard this remark and was encouraged

20

by it to approach his mother with an offer that he made in a hoarse whisper.

"I don't mind helpin' judge the cakes," he said. "I mean I'll taste 'em an' tell the people what they taste like, then it'll save 'em the trouble of tastin' em. I'm only thinkin' of savin' them trouble. . . ."

"Of course not, William," said his mother firmly.

She had put the cakes on a plate on the trestle table and by it a card bearing her name and address. William looked at the cakes. They were small but very delicious-looking, the top of each decorated by a preserved cherry. William adored preserved cherries.

"May I have jus' *one* for helping you bring them?"

"No, William, of course not," said his mother, "and you didn't help bring them."

William had recourse to his sardonic laugh again.

"Huh! *Well*," he said, gazing about the room, "seems funny to me to make all this stuff just for badges an' people that would sooner be without it. I 'spect it'll *kill* someone at the Cottage Hospital an' then you'll all get into trouble an'," darkly, "don't say I didn't warn you."

His mother promised that she wouldn't, and they set off homeward with the empty basket.

The next morning William had completely forgotten the competition in the Village Hall. It was Saturday, and he rose gaily to a day of glorious freedom.

He spent the morning in the woods playing Red Indians with his Outlaws, but in the afternoon time began to hang heavily on his hands. Ginger had reluctantly gone under escort to pay a visit to his dentist; Douglas, also reluctantly, was staying at home to receive a visit from his godmother; and Henry had been forbidden to come out owing to the state in which he had arrived home after the morning's Red Indian game, in the process of which he had rolled into a stream with William, and, unfortunately for him, William had happened to be on top.

21

William therefore was left to his own devices. He didn't feel in the mood for his own devices and wandered aimlessly down the road hoping to meet a kindred spirit. The spirit he met, however, was far from being a kindred one. It was the spirit of Hubert Lane, who had been the bitter foe of the Outlaws from time, to the Outlaws, immemorial. Or rather it was the body of Hubert Lane, for Hubert Lane was fat and sly and possessed much discretion but very little spirit. The feud between Hubert Lane and the Outlaws happened to be passing through a quiescent period, so William merely passed Hubert with a hostile grimace. At least William tried to pass Hubert with a hostile grimace. But the grimace, beginning splendidly as a hideous facial contortion expressive of hatred and defiance, faded away, despite all William's endeavours, into a sheepish grin. For Hubert Lane was not alone. He was accompanied by a little girl of about his own age, but of very different appearance—a little girl with dark eyes, dark curly hair, and smooth dimpled cheeks. An indisputably attractive little girl. A little girl of whom he was obviously unworthy to be the companion. William slackened his pace. The little girl slackened hers.

"Ask that boy," William heard her say to Hubert.

"Him!" said Hubert with a scorn that brought the lust of battle to William's heart, "not likely."

"But why not, Hubert?" persisted the little girl. "He might know. He might have a watch. And it's silly not knowing the time."

"I'm not going to ask *him*," said Hubert again in a tone that inflamed still further the lust of battle in William's heart.

"I will, then," said the little girl. She turned suddenly and came towards William, who was standing in the middle of the road, wholly absorbed apparently in the contemplation of the horizon.

"Please, boy," she said distantly, "could you tell us the time? Hubert came out without his watch and I've

22

not got one yet. I'm going to have one when I'm twelve."

William looked at her as if realising her presence with a start.

"I beg your pardon," he said with excessive politeness, "I din' see you. I was jus' thinkin' about somethin'." He said this in order that she should not suspect that he had stopped in order to look after her. "I often do that," he went on garrulously, "stand an' think a bit in the road."

But the little girl was not interested in William's power of thought.

"Can you tell us the time, please?" she said impatiently.

"Oh yes," said William, determined to prolong the conversation to its utmost limits. "Yes, I c'n tell you the time all right." He felt leisurely in his jacket pocket. "Got my watch here, all right, I expect. . . . No, it doesn't seem to be here. I expect it's in the other pocket." He felt exhaustively in the other pocket. "What's your name?" he said conversationally as he searched.

"Dorinda," said the little girl still impatiently.

"Mine's William," volunteered William.

She betrayed no interest in this fact—only said shortly:

"Isn't your watch in that pocket?"

"No, it doesn't seem to be," said William in a tone of great surprise. "Funny thing it not bein' in either of these pockets. I 'spect it's in my trouser pocket."

He began a lengthy search in a trouser pocket, saying meanwhile:

"Where do you live?"

"In Godalming," said the little girl. "I'm Hubert's cousin, and I've come to spend the day with them."

It was evident that she did not offer this information with any idea of reciprocating William's friendly overtures. She spoke curtly. her frowning gaze fixed

23

on the spot where William's hand was still engaged in its shameless search for a non-existent watch.

"It *can't* be in that pocket," she went on with distinct annoyance in her tone, "if you haven't found it yet."

"No," agreed William confidingly, "I was jus' beginnin' to think it couldn't. I'll have a look in the other. How long are you staying?"

"Only to-day. Well, it can't be in that one either, can it?"

"I 'spose not," agreed William reluctantly, "but I thought I might have a good look while I was about it. There's my waistcoat pockets yet, I'll have a good look in all of those now."

But the little girl had lightly slipped her fingers one after the other into his waistcoat pockets before he had realised what she was doing.

"It's not in those either," she said.

"I must have lost it," said William trying to assume the anguished expression of one who has just discovered the loss of a valuable watch. "It mus' have dropped out of my pocket on to the road as I came along. Tell you what, I'll walk back with you 'n' try 'n' find it."

Delighted with the ruse, he set off with the little girl towards Hubert, who stood several yards away from them with an expression of patient aloofness on his fat and pallid countenance.

"He's lost his watch, Hubert," she explained. "He thinks he must have dropped it somewhere on the road. He's coming back with us to find out."

Hubert turned his small malignant eyes upon William.

"He's not got a watch," he said.

William temporised as best he could in the face of this undoubted truth.

"Huh!" he said, "a lot you know about it."

"I know you've not got one."

"Oh, do you," said William sarcastically. "Well,

24

you know a bit too much. Let *me* tell *you* my aunt gave me one for Christmas."

"Yes, and you tried to make a bomb out of it last week with some gunpowder, and a lot of things in your house got blown up, and there wasn't any of the watch left at all, and your father said you'd not to have another till you were twenty-one even if anyone gave you one."

"Whoever told you a silly tale like that?" said William, but he spoke feebly, knowing that to Hubert's companion the story must bear the stamp of truth.

"I'll prove it to you," said Hubert in his most superior tone. "Our cook's your cook's sister an' she was in your house when it happened. An' she said you got into a jolly row—so there!"

"She was makin' it up, pullin' your leg," said William, but he spoke without any serious hope of convincing either of them.

They had been walking slowly and had just come to a bend in the road.

"There's the church clock," cried Dorinda suddenly, "so it's all right, and it doesn't matter about his watch." She addressed William with haughty politeness. "Good-bye, an' I'm sorry we troubled you."

"Oh, *that's* all right," said William effusively, "that's quite all right. It wasn't any trouble at all. Not at all. I *like* takin' trouble for people. Well, I happen to be goin' this way so I'll walk along with you, shall I?"

Their silence quite obviously did not give consent, but William was of tougher metal than to be quelled by a snub. He joined them, walking on the other side of Dorinda, and raised his voice pleasantly in conversation.

"I can tell you some jolly interestin' things," he said. "I can tell you lots of things you don't know about Red Indians and pirates and smugglers and stag-beetles and wasps and caterpillars and huntin' wild beasts and things like that."

They ignored him. Dorinda presented the back of her head to him, turning her face to Hubert.

"*Do* go on, Hubert," she said enthusiastically. "Tell me more about that place you went to last holidays."

"Munich?" drawled Hubert loftily. "It's in Germany, you know. I picked up quite a lot of German there."

"I could tell you things I've done you'd hardly believe," announced William. "Fightin' Red Indians an' catchin' pirates an' things like that."

In his imaginary adventures William identified himself sometimes with the Red Indians and pirates and sometimes with their attackers. Whichever side he led, of course, conquered. But the little girl took no notice of him. Her head remained turned away from him to Hubert.

"Tell me more about Munich, Hubert," she pleaded.

"We went to see art galleries and museums and things," said Hubert, "and"—his small eyes suddenly glistening—"we stayed at a hotel where they gave us jolly decent food."

There was, as William saw it, only one thing to do and he did it. He stepped back, then suddenly inserted himself between Hubert and Dorinda, so that Dorinda's eager smiling face was turned to him.

"I can tell you some jolly interesting things about smugglers, too," he said.

But Hubert, after an ineffectual attempt to push him back, had gone round to Dorinda's other side, and Dorinda at once turned to him, presenting to William again a cold quarter profile.

"Tell me some things you saw there, Hubert."

"Oh, I saw a lot of things," said Hubert grandly, "statues and things."

"What sort of statues?"

William tried to repeat the ruse, but Hubert was prepared for it and braced his stout body to resist the passage of William's between him and Dorinda.

"Oh, kings and people," said Hubert, digging an

elbow hard into William's stomach, "and there's a sort of palace where a sort of king used to live and a big bridge with a river underneath and——"

His voice died away. After the attack on his stomach William had fallen back, but he was now walking on Hubert's heels, and Hubert despite himself was beginning to hurry.

He still talked to Dorinda, but somewhat disconnectedly.

"And—there's—a sort—of—garden. Ow!"

"Why are you walking so fast, Hubert?"

"I'm not. It's—*Ow!*"

Suddenly it was William who was next to her.

"What sort of books do you like best?" said William. William had realised with reluctance that she was not interested in pirates and smugglers and had decided to try another subject. He had, while spending a day in bed with a cold last month, read a book whose plot he meant to recount to her—a plot of hauntings and murders and arch criminals and fights in the dark and wild pursuits over land and sea, a plot in fact after his own heart.

She was taken aback by William's sudden appearance and had answered his question before she had realised that it was he who had put it.

"Fairy tales," she said, then turned at once to Hubert who had betaken himself to her other side. "What sort of a garden, Hubert?"

"Oh—a sort of—a garden just like an English garden," said Hubert.

"I'm jolly good at magic myself," said William modestly. That arrested her. She turned to him slowly.

"You can't be," she said, "only magicians are good at magic."

"Well, I'm a magician," said William. His tone of finality and certitude was rather impressive. Dorinda looked at him incredulous, but interested.

"You!" she said.

"He's not a magician," said Hubert. "I can tell you that."

"Oh, aren't I?" said William meaningly.

"Well, you tell me one bit of magic you've ever done," challenged Hubert.

"I made a trifle and some cakes come out of nothing in a cupboard at a party of yours," said William.

He referred to a dramatic occasion when, having looked through the window and seen Hubert hiding the trifle and cakes before his party so that he and his cronies could consume them alone afterwards, he had concealed his knowledge till the middle of tea, then pretended to produce them from their hiding-place by magic.

Hubert sheered away quickly from this reference.

"Oh that!" he said, "that was nothing. You're no more a magician than I am."

"All right, do something then if *you're* a magician. Turn something into something."

"I'd do it as well as you could, anyway."

"All right. Do it."

"*Both* turn something into something," said Dorinda excitedly. "Hubert, do it first."

"Well, I bet I can do anything he can," said Hubert, "it was him that said he was a magician. I only said I was as much one as he was considering he wasn't one at all."

But Dorinda was thrilled by the idea and refused to abandon it.

"Both *try* to do magic, anyway," she said. "I tell you what, I'm frightfully hungry, and in the fairy tale I was reading last night, when the princess began to get frightfully hungry, the magician commanded a large room full of food to appear, and it did. You do that, Hubert. Say 'I command a large room full of food to appear,' and see if it does."

"I command a large room full of food to appear," said Hubert, and added impatiently: "Of course it won't. I knew it wouldn't."

Dorinda had to admit rather regretfully that it hadn't.

"Now let William try," she said.

"Yes," sneered Hubert, "let William try an' see if he does it any better. It's him that said he was a magician."

An idea had come to William. "I can't do it jus' this minute," he said. "I'll do it when I get jus' by that lamppost. My magic's always strongest when I'm near a lamppost."

They walked to the lamppost, Dorinda watching him eagerly, Hubert sniggering.

He stood by the lamppost opposite the door of the Village Hall and said: "I command a big room full of food to appear."

Then he flung open the door of the Village Hall.

In a large room empty of human beings stood trestle tables laden with cakes and jam and bottled fruits and other delicacies. Hubert's eyes protruded in amazement. Hubert's mother had no dealings with the Women's Guild and he had heard nothing of the Cookery Exhibition in the Village Hall. The little girl clasped her hands and gasped.

"Oh; how wonderful!"

Triumph filled William's heart, then slowly ebbed away leaving apprehension.

"I'm afraid it's magic food," he said to the little girl, "you can't axshully *eat* it. There's a spell laid on it that my magic's not strong enough to take off."

But the little girl was already at the cake table munching energetically.

"But it *is*, William," she said indistinctly, "it *has* taken it off. I *can* eat it."

Hubert, who was never backward when food was in sight, had joined her, and already the dishes of cakes were beginning to diminish. Some of them bore little labels with the legends, "First prize," "Second prize," "Third prize," but they ignored these. Hubert, who had a passion for jam, crossed over to the jam table

and emptied several pots of jam in the space of a few
minutes. William, thinking that, as he would be
blamed for the crime, he might as well share in its
profits, found the dish of his mother's cakes (it bore a

*"I'm afraid it's magic food," said William. "You
can't eat it."*

label Highly Commended) and ate them all. He found
them very good but on the whole less enjoyable than
in the raw state.

"Well, that was a *lovely* magic meal," said the little
girl at last, "but I couldn't eat any more so let's go
now."

Hubert, who had eaten one jar of jam too many,
expressed himself also ready to go.

William threw an anxious glance round the room. Several of the dishes were quite empty. He moved a few cakes from other dishes on to them, put the empty jars of jam under the table, and hoped for the best.

But the little girl was already at the table. "I can eat it,"
she said.

They went out, and William drew a sigh of relief when he found the village street as empty as the Hall. No one had seen them go in. No one had seen them go out. The crime might after all not be discovered. They walked on.

Dorinda, insatiable as all her sex, demanded from William further proof of his magic power. She asked him to turn the lamppost into a prince in a cloak of gold and a diamond crown. William informed her rather curtly that his supply of magic was only sufficient for one spell a day. She accepted the explanation quite simply, obviously believing implicitly in his magic powers. Hubert was bewildered and annoyed. Dorinda ignored him. It was evident that no one existed for Dorinda except William. She questioned him eagerly and unceasingly about his magic powers. Hubert, after enduring this for several minutes, made a bold bid for her attention.

"I can tell you a lot more about Munich," he said, "there's a big lake just near it where——"

"Do be quiet," said Dorinda. "I'm not a bit interested in the silly place."

"But you said you were," he protested.

"That was only because we'd got to write an essay on the place where we'd spent our holidays, and I thought I'd get more marks if I'd spent it abroad."

"But you didn't," said Hubert.

"No, silly, but if I wrote about the place you were talking about she'd think I had, wouldn't she? But it sounded a stupid place—*heaps* stupider than Swanage, so I'm going to stick to Swanage after all. . . ." She turned to William: "And can you do anything you like with your spell?"

"Well, some days it's stronger than others," said William anxious to guard against future contingencies. "Some days it's quite weak and I can only do *very* little things with it."

"It was *very* strong to-day wasn't it?" said Dorinda with a sigh of blissful reminiscence. "I've never tasted such nice cakes before."

William remembered with an apprehensive qualm that Dorinda had eaten the entire contents of the dish that bore the label "Special Award of Honour." She had an appetite that her appearance of graceful fragility somehow did not suggest. William had filled up the dish with cakes from other exhibits, but he had an uneasy conviction that the matter would not end there.

"Anyone could *tell* they were magic cakes by the taste of them," went on Dorinda fervently.

Then Hubert brought out the bombshell he had been carefully preparing.

"I did laugh when I saw you running away from Farmer Jenks' bull the other day," he said casually to William.

William was taken aback. He certainly had fled precipitately when he realised that Farmer Jenks' bull was in the field with him, but he had not known that there was a witness of his flight. Hubert had seen him and was keeping the story till it could be used most effectively against him.

"Well," he said indignantly, "*everyone* runs away from a bull."

"I don't," said Hubert.

"Oh don't you!" said William. "Well I've seen you." Memory came to his aid. "I saw you in this *very* field, an' as soon as you saw that the bull was in it and coming to you, you ran into that shed and shut the door an' hid in it."

Hubert laughed.

"That was all you saw, wasn't it? You didn't see me come out of the shed and chase the bull across the field, did you?"

"No, I didn't."

"Well, that's what I did after you'd gone on."

"Well, why did you run into the shed, then?"

"Jus' to lure it on. To make it come right up to the shed door after me so that I could burst out at it an' chase it right across the field."

There was no doubt that Hubert had an imagination that almost rivalled William's in fertility, and there was no doubt that Dorinda was unduly (as William considered in this case) credulous.

"Oh, Hubert, *did* you?" she said.

"Yes," said Hubert.

33

B

"I didn't see you," put in William.

"No 'cause you'd gone on. I waited till you'd gone on."

"An' you chased it *right* across the field, Hubert?" said Dorinda admiringly.

It was obvious that she had quite forgotten William's powers of magic in this new thrill of Hubert's powers of bullchasing. It was not William's first lesson in the fickleness of woman.

"Yes," said Hubert with his unbearable swagger.

"And was it really this field?" said Dorinda.

"Yes," said Hubert.

"And was that the shed?" said Dorinda pointing to a small shed in a corner of the field.

"Yes," said Hubert.

William looked round. A thick-set animal was making its way across the field in their direction.

"And that's the bull," he said.

Without a moment's hesitation the three of them took to their heels and fled across to the shed. There came behind them as they ran the thud of pounding hoofs. They slammed the door of the shed and bolted it. From beneath the door came the sound of heavy breathing. They could see a fraction of the nostril of their foe beneath it as he made vain efforts to get to his victims. Hubert's face had assumed a sea-green tint. William was panting. Only Dorinda was serene, untroubled. She turned to Hubert with the eager smile of one to whom the best is yet to come.

"You've lured him to the shed, Hubert," she said, "now go out and chase him across the field."

There was no sarcasm in her tone. She had firmly believed Hubert's story. It had never once occurred to her that their flight was not in the nature of a ruse in order to give Hubert the chance of chasing the bull across the field again.

"Go on, Hubert," she said, "go out and chase him."

She was dancing about in her eager anticipation of the joy of watching Hubert chase the bull.

"Chase him like you chased him the other day," she said. "Hurry up. He's still outside. I can hear him. Throw open the door and give him a fright and chase him right across the field. I'm *longing* for it."

Hubert turned his sea-green face to her.

"Don't be such a fool," he said.

Her eager excitement died away.

"Aren't you *going* to, Hubert?" she said.

"Course I'm not."

Disillusion clouded the blue eyes. She spoke in a small sad voice.

"Hubert, didn't you—didn't you chase it the other time?"

"Course I didn't," snapped Hubert.

Then suddenly his fat sea-green face broke up. "Boo hoo!" he sobbed, "I'm frightened. You oughtn't ever to have let me come into this field. It's all your fault. Boo hoo!"

Dorinda stared at him in amazement. Then she turned to William and something of her glow returned.

"*You'll* do it, William, won't you?" she said.

"What?" said William feebly.

"Chase him away. You know you said you'd fought smugglers. A bull isn't *half* as much trouble to fight as smugglers."

She gazed at him eagerly, imploringly, and yet with something of apprehension, as if having once tasted disillusionment she couldn't be quite sure of not tasting it again.

William looked at the sea-green blubbing face of Hubert and felt suddenly that any fate was preferable to that of sharing in its shame, of bringing the crestfallen look of disillusionment again into Dorinda's blue eyes.

"All right," he said airily, "I'll go 'n' chase him all right."

Without stopping for a second to consider his decision, he opened the door, stepped out and closed it behind him. He was alone in the field facing the bull.

To his surprise the bull did not attack him at once. It curvetted about for a few moments, then wheeled round suddenly and went pounding back across the field. William's rôle was open to him and he fulfilled it instinctively. He set off at a run, and Dorinda and Hubert, who had opened the door, beheld the amazing spectacle of William pursuing the bull across the field. Half-way across, the bull stopped and faced him, again curvetted heavily, then wheeled round and set off at a run again. William followed. The gate leading from the field to the farm yard was open. The bull disappeared into the farm yard. William pursued it to the gate, where he was stopped by the sudden appearance of Farmer Jenks' youngest daughter, a damsel of pleasing appearance with none of her father's surliness of disposition. She smiled pleasantly at William.

"Father *will* be mad that you've found out," she said.

"Found out what?" said William breathless from his run.

"About Sammy."

"Who's Sammy?" said William.

"The bull," laughed the damsel. "You see, his mother died when he was born, and we girls have brought him up, and he's as sweet tempered as a lamb, and loves a romp like a puppy. But father always wants you boys to think he's fierce, 'cause of keeping you out of his fields. How did you find out?"

William collected his scattered forces and assumed a knowing and superior air.

"Oh, I know a lot about bulls," he said. "I can always tell whether bulls are fierce or not," and added hastily, not wishing to lose the credit for superhuman valour in claiming that of superhuman knowledge: "Not that I'm afraid of any ole bull however savage it is. I jus' get hold of their horns and twist 'em on to the ground by 'em so's they can't move."

The girl laughed, and gave him an apple, and told him to get out of the field quick before father came

36

home. Then she shut the gate and disappeared. William swaggered back across the field to where Dorinda, starry eyed and ecstatic, and Hubert, still sea-green and blubbing, were coming from the shed to meet him. He presented the apple to Dorinda with a courtly air.

"Oh William," she sighed blissfully, "it was *lovely* to watch you. I *knew* you would. What was the girl saying to you?"

"She was telling me what a jolly fierce bull it was, and that no one had ever chased it before," said William.

They walked home slowly, and William beguiled the time by describing from imagination other and more terrific encounters with bulls in which he somewhat monotonously played the part of hero. Hubert recovered from his epilepsy of fear, and began to explain that he would have chased the bull himself if he hadn't had cramp in his leg, and that he'd just been on the point of going out to chase it when William had forestalled him. Dorinda ignored him, demanding still more stories from the heroic William. Her credulity and his imagination were well matched.

They had retraced their steps to the Village Hall. William's instinct was to slink past it as inconspicuously as possible, but Dorinda expressed surprise to see it still standing there.

"I should have thought that it would have vanished as soon as we'd finished with it," she said. "Let's go in and see if there's any of the magic food left. I'm quite hungry again."

Reluctantly William followed her into the Hall. The scene was not the peaceful scene that usually met the eyes and ears of visitors to the Women's Guild Exhibitions. The sounds of fierce reproaches rent the air. A tall athletic-looking woman was angrily brandishing an empty jam jar (one of Hubert's efforts), which she had found under the table, and shouting at the top of her voice. Others brandished prize tickets and dishes, also shouting at the tops of their voices. The scene was chaotic.

Most of their anger seemed to be directed against a woman in a blue overall wearing a steward's badge, who was standing at bay against a trestle table, defending herself hysterically.

"No, I've no explanation. I don't know how it happened. Yes, I was left alone in charge for an hour just before it opened. Yes, I did leave it for a short time . . . well, I only just slipped down to the chemist. They shouldn't have made me judge the pickles . . . pickles never did suit me . . . I was in *agony*. I only went for some bicarbonate of soda. I didn't stay long . . . not very long. He had to go upstairs to his store room for some . . . No, I didn't lock the door when I was away . . . no one was about and I only meant to be away a second and one can't think of everything and I was in *agony*. No, I didn't notice anything wrong when I got back. No, of course I didn't examine everything. It was almost time to open the door and I was still in agony. I still *am* in agony. I think he'd had the stuff in stock too long, it didn't seem to have any effect on me at all. I shall be a wreck for life after this . . . some of the pickled onions were practically *raw*. How *can* I tell you what happened . . . ? I don't *know* what happened. . . ." She stopped for breath and an angry babel of voices broke out again.

"Here's my cakes on a dish with a first prize label with someone else's name on. My cakes got first prize and they've made a mistake in the name."

"Pardon *me*, it's *my* name and the prize is for *my* cakes."

"Well, where *are* your cakes?"

"The person who took them away should know that."

"How *dare* you! . . . You never sent in any cakes. You forged a prize ticket."

The raging individual with the empty jam jar pushed them on one side and took the stage.

"*Slaved* over it I did! Best jam for miles around! Everyone says so! *Sure* of the prize, I was. And where do I find it? Emptied and stuck under a table. I'll find who did it if I die, and I'll have their eyes out. There's been some dirty work here and——"

A scream interrupted her. Hubert had thoughtfully filled his every pocket with cakes and biscuits on his previous visit to the Hall. Feeling hungry and shaken and quite unaware of the meaning of the uproar around him, he now absently took out a cake and began to munch it. A woman standing near him recognised her missing masterpiece and raised a scream. They fell upon Hubert and emptied his pockets. Hubert had a good eye for pastries and every one of the cakes they took from him had been a prize winner. Each one was greeted with screams of anguished recognition by its creator. Chaos and babel were redoubled. Hubert in terror twisted himself from the hold of his captors, and fled out of the Hall followed by a crowd of enraged women. The uproar died away in the distance. Peace descended upon the Hall with its small crowd of disinterested non-exhibitors who had merely come to see the exhibition. And soon another sensation ran through the company like fire among stubble set going by a careless word of Dorinda's. It was the sensation of William and the bull. The story increased in picturesqueness and variation as it spread from mouth to mouth. Dorinda herself had confused several of the details of what actually happened with details of the imaginary bull exploits that William had related to her on the way home.

According to one rumour William had seized hold of the horns of the bull just as it was going to toss him, and, being flung upon its back by the toss, had kept his seat there and guided the animal back to the farm yard. According to another he had wrestled with it. According to another he had quelled it with the power of the human eye. According to another he had been gored horribly and was now lying at the point

39

of death in the Cottage Hospital. The sight of his extremely healthy figure had a depressing effect on this rumour, but, as he could not be seen by everyone in the room at once, did not actually kill it. An eager and credulous crowd surrounded him, demanding details. He gave them freely. Then, just as he was describing how the bull had slunk through the gate of the field with its tail between its legs after he had wrestled with it and thrown it, he heard the sound of the returning crowd of exhibitors and decided that the moment had come for him to take his departure. Dorinda followed him.

"Why are you running so fast, William?" she said, trying to keep up with him.

"Jus' 'cause I like runnin'," said William breathlessly.

When he had reached a safe distance from the Village Hall he stopped.

"What were all those people making such a noise about?" said Dorinda.

"Oh, they jus' like makin' a noise," said William.

"I expect they were *frightfully* grateful to you for making all that magic food for them, weren't they?"

"I expect so," said William.

"I expect that was what they were all so excited about," said Dorinda; "I wonder where Hubert is?"

"He went for a little run too," said William.

"By himself?"

"Yes."

"I don't care. I'd rather be without him. I like you *heaps* better than Hubert."

"An' I like you heaps better than most girls I know," said William.

They had reached the end of the road where Hubert's house stood.

"I've got to go now," said Dorinda regretfully. "I'm only staying here to-day you know. Father's fetching me after tea an' it must be tea-time now."

"Well good-bye," said William brusquely.

"Good-bye, William. I think you're the bravest person in the world, and I think your magic's *wonderful* and I love you *ever* so much."

She raised her face and kissed him. She was unexpectedly pleasant to kiss. Then she waved her hand and disappeared down the lane.

William went on. He had decided to go for a long walk. Probably the leading part he had played in the Women's Guild Cookery Exhibition had been discovered by now, and it would be as well to keep out of the way in case instruments of justice were already searching for him. He hoped that the story of his exploit with the bull would have the effect of tempering justice with mercy, but he didn't really care. He thought of Dorinda's gaze of admiration, of her unexpectedly pleasant kiss, of the delicious feast of prize home-made cakes, of Hubert, sea-green and blubbing, of the fascinating feeling of pursuing a bull across a field . . . and he felt that nothing on earth could take the savour from these memories.

He took a stick from the hedge and swaggered along the road, singing loudly to himself and slashing the stick through the air.

In front of him fled thousands of imaginary bulls, their tails between their legs.

CHAPTER III

THE OUTLAWS AND THE MISSIONARY

It was Mrs. Monks, the Vicar's wife, who insisted on holding a drawing-room missionary meeting for children the day after she had held the drawing-room missionary meeting for grown-ups. She was a woman whose zeal sometimes outran her discretion, and she was also a frugal woman who did not like to see good

41

cakes and sandwiches wasted. She approached the Outlaws' parents first of all, and the Outlaws' parents, though not enthusiastic, could not bring any valid reason against her proposal. Their lack of enthusiasm was due to a conviction, born of experience, that things in which their sons took part generally ended disastrously, rather than to any definite flaw in the project itself.

"But how *can* it do any harm?" said Mrs. Monks. "They'll come to tea, and he'll just talk to them and ask them *all* to try to collect some money, and then he'll have another meeting in a fortnight's time and they can give in their money."

So the Outlaws' parents reluctantly acquiesced, and four brushed and scoured boys went to swell the ranks of Mrs. Monks's juvenile missionary meeting.

"Waste of an afternoon," grumbled William moodily.

"There'll be tea anyway," said Ginger, trying to look on the bright side.

"Yes, what they left yesterday," said William, "an' it'll all be stale, an' not enough, an' she'll not give us any more. I know her. The last eatin' up tea I came to of hers I only got one piece of bread and butter, an' it was as hard as nails, an' all curled up."

"*An'* listenin' to a dull ole lecture all the time," said Ginger. "I'm *sick* of lectures. It's only a week ago we had one on stars at school an' I was too far back to hear a word he said, an' those that could said I was jolly lucky."

But the gloomy forebodings of the Outlaws were not justified. The tea was ample and the lecturer not only audible but inspiring. He stirred the competitive instinct that is such a potent factor with the young. He ended his speech by saying: "You must each try to collect two shillings, but you mustn't stop at the two shillings, you know. Now let us see which of all you boys and girls can bring me the most money to our next meeting."

And at once the Outlaws felt that their honour demanded that they should beat all the other competitors and bring the largest amount of money to the next meeting. It didn't matter whether it was a question of good deeds or ill, of success in trespassing or fighting or missionary work, the Outlaws liked to lord it over their contemporaries.

They went straight to the old barn to discuss the matter. William was the only one of them who had any money, and he had fourpence, but he lost no time in informing them that his fourpence was not eligible as the nucleus of their new fund.

"I'd saved it for a new pistol," he explained, "one like Victor Jameson's got. They're only fourpence but they'd sold the last one to Victor, but the man said he was havin' some more in an'" (putting the fourpence very firmly back into his pocket) "an' this fourpence is for the pistol when it comes, not for any ole savages. I'd 've spent it las' Saturday if he'd had a pistol in the shop, so I count it as spent 'cause it's only waitin' till the pistols come in."

The Outlaws admitted the justice of this.

"Yes, it wouldn't be fair to take your fourpence," said Ginger. "We'll get enough without that. We'll find some way of makin' money we've never tried before."

Their previous attempts at money-making had indeed been numerous but not strikingly successful.

"We've tried everything," said William. "We've tried shows and sellin' things to people an' doin' things for people, an' actin' plays an' writin' newspapers an' —an' everythin'. I don't think there is any way of makin' money that we've not tried."

"My aunt was readin' a story to me las' Sunday," said Henry. "I wasn't listenin' but I couldn't help hearin' bits now an' then an' it was about a girl that wanted some money for her sister that was starvin' an' she sold her hair."

"Her *what*?" said William incredulously.

"We've come to sell you our hair," said William.
"We'll sell it for five pounds the lot."

"Her hair."

"Who to?"

"A hairdresser."

"Well!" said William amazed, "I never heard of anyone doin' that before. How much did he give for it."

"Five pounds," said Henry.

"Five—*what*!" said William.

"Five pounds."

"Crumbs!"

"It *must* be true if it's in a book," said Henry.

"Well, it's a jolly easy way of gettin' money if it's true," said William. "Let's go 'n' try it. I say! Three fives are fifteen. What if he gives us fifteen pounds!"

Credulous as the Outlaws were, this hardly seemed possible, but they were not prepared for the ridicule with which Mr. Theobald, the village barber, received their offer.

"We've come to sell you our hair," said William.

"*What?*" said Mr. Theobald.

"We'll sell you our hair. Five pounds the lot," said William generously, "the ordin'ry price is five pounds each, but we don't want to be mean, so we'll sell it at five pounds the lot."

Mr. Theobald threw back his bald head and roared with laughter. He went into his little saloon and told it to his customers. He went to his front door and proclaimed it to the village street.

"I'll cut it for sixpence each," he said to the Outlaws at the end, "and not before it needs it either."

Loud laughter followed the Outlaws out of the shop. Loud laughter followed them down the village street. The joke was repeated from door to door. They heard Mr. Theobald repeating it in a raucous voice for the benefit of the further end of the village street. The doubled shouts of laughter accompanied them. The Outlaws marched on, their faces flaming angrily. They did not take kindly to being butts for ridicule.

In the old barn they sat down and considered this new complication that had invaded the situation.

"You know what he is when he gets hold of anything he thinks is funny," said William; "he'll tell it to everyone who goes into his shop an' everyone'll be laughing at us. All your aunt's fault," he ended moodily to Henry, "reading you stories that weren't true."

"Well, what're we goin' to *do*?" said Ginger.

The problem of wiping out this insult now filled the whole mental horizon of the Outlaws. They had quite

45

forgotten the project for which they had wanted the money.

"We've gotter do somethin' to make people laugh at *him*," muttered Henry.

William thought of Mr. Theobald—saw him in his mind's eye standing as he stood every morning in his shop doorway, the sun shining on his bald head, beneath his sign: "THEOBALD HAIRDRESSER."

And William's face was lit suddenly as by a light from within.

"I know what we'll do," he said, "we only want a bit of black paint and a ladder, and there's both in our toolshed."

The next morning the men who hurried down the village street towards the station went shaking and guffawing on their way. For Mr. Theobald stood in his doorway as usual, the sun shining on his bald head. But William and the Outlaws had come after dark with a ladder and a pot of black paint, and the sign above his head now ran: "THE BALD HAIR-DRESSER." Mr. Theobald was not annoyed by the laughter. He was still engaged in broadcasting the story of the Outlaws' offer and he took the laughter as tribute to the jest.

It was not till almost lunch time that he realised that the laughter that still resounded through the village street was connected in any way with himself.

That little affair settled, the Outlaws turned their attention again to the matter of the money for the missionaries. If Mr. Theobald would not buy their hair, they must find some other way of making money. They discussed every method they could think of, and dismissed each as impossible. They had almost given up hope when Douglas found a page of his mother's cookery book on the floor of the dining-room, and, picking it up, began to read it simply because at the time he happened to have nothing else to do.

At once he summoned another meeting of the Outlaws in the old barn.

"Look," he said eagerly, "it tells you how to make ginger beer an' it sounds quite easy. An' *everyone* likes ginger beer. I bet if we make ginger beer an' sell it, we'll get a lot of money."

"How do you make it?" said William.

"You only want ginger an' water an' sugar an' lemon an' yeast," he said, and ended simply, "an' they're all things we can get from our homes without anyone knowin' they've gone."

The Outlaws took up the idea with enthusiasm. It was decided that Ginger should get the yeast from his home, Henry the sugar, Douglas the ginger, and William the lemon.

"An' we'll start collectin' bottles at once," said William. "I bet we ought to make enough to conquer all the savages in the world."

Despite the eloquence of the missionary, the Outlaws were still somewhat vague as to his exact aims.

A motley crew of bottles was assembled in the old barn, and the Outlaws viewed them with pride.

"I best we'll get more money this way than anyone," said William optimistically. "I bet we'll keep on doin' it afterwards too an' have a bit of money for ourselves for a change. An' then when we're grown up we can have a ginger beer shop an' I bet we end up as millionaires."

Ginger, who had purloined a basin from home, was already engaged upon the manufacture.

"I'm puttin' a *lot* of yeast in," he said, "because that's what makes it fizzy."

It was a proud moment for the Outlaws when they stood by the roadside, their strange assortment of bottles displayed on a board, with a notice "Ginger beer tuppence a bottel. Made by us," elegantly designed in paints of many colours by Henry. It was by no means the first time that the Outlaws had had a stall by the roadside, but it was the first time that they had actually manufactured the wares they were selling. There was no lack of customers, and the bottles of ginger beer had all gone in less than an hour. In fact, the Outlaws were already manufacturing another supply in the old barn, when the crowd of enraged customers ran them to earth, demanding their money back. It appeared that all the bottles had exploded either on the way home or as soon as they reached home. One customer had been hit in the eye by the cork. Another had had her coat ruined. The father of another had been caught by a piece of flying glass. The cat of another had been so terrified by the report that it had shot out of the house like an arrow from a bow and so far all search for it had proved fruitless. The baby brother of another had been drenched in ginger beer. The fact that he had been intensely amused by the episode and had called out "'gain!" detracted nothing from his mother's indignation. One cork had smashed an electric-light bulb and another a valuable vase. Had the customers come back alone the Outlaws might possibly have been a match for them, but they didn't. They brought indignant parents in their train—the parents whose vases and bulbs had been broken and whose babies had been drenched in ginger beer. The parents did not merely demand the money back. They extracted it violently from the Outlaws' pockets, telling them many forcible home truths in the process.

When they had gone, the Outlaws sat and looked at each other blankly. "Well," said William bitterly, "talk about *savages*!"

Then he turned out his pocket and found the four pennies still intact.

"Wonder they didn't take *that* while they were about it," he said ironically, "well, nothin' on *earth'd* make me give missionaries these four pennies now."

Henry turned his sorrowful gaze to the mixture that stood in a corner of the old barn.

"What're we goin' to do with that?" he said.

"Tell you what," said Douglas, "let's try my aunt. I bet she doesn't like ginger beer, but she's jolly keen

48

on missionaries an' savages an' things like that. She's gone away to-day, but she'll be back to-morrow afternoon. We'll take 'em round to-morrow afternoon."

To-morrow afternoon was the afternoon of the meeting, and the Outlaws felt that it was running it rather close, but their usual optimism upheld them, and they set off hopefully, early the next afternoon, to Douglas's aunt's house with a wheelbarrow full of bottles.

Douglas's aunt disliked boys and was on far from friendly terms with Douglas, but she was, as Douglas had said, "keen on missionaries an' savages an' things like that," and she was deeply touched by their errand.

"I think it's splendid of you, boys," she said, "and I do hope that it means that your conduct's going to be *completely* different in the future. I do hope that, now you've turned your thoughts and interest to *serious* things, we shan't have so much to complain of in you. This is a *very* good sign, and I'm only too glad to give my subscription to the Cause through you."

She opened her purse and gave William three half-crowns.

"I don't really want the mixture, of course, so you'd better put it in the greenhouse to be out of the way."

They put it in the greenhouse, and went quickly away. A muffled report from the greenhouse, followed by the sound of breaking glass, reached them as they shut the gate.

"Seven an' six," said William blissfully, when they had reached a safe distance from Douglas's aunt's house, "I bet no one'll have more than that."

Victor Jameson passed on the other side of the street.

"Hi!" called William, "how much have you got for the savages?"

"Seven an' six," called Victor proudly, "an' I bet you've not got more'n that."

"Oh, *haven't* we?" returned William, but the faces of the Outlaws had fallen.

They waited till Victor was out of earshot, then Ginger said:

"Well, we won't have the most after all."

"Yes, we jolly well will," said William firmly, "*an'* we won't use my fourpence either."

"How'll we do it?" demanded Ginger.

"We'll have to think out some way," said William the unconquerable.

At that moment another group of boys passed. They too had been at the missionary meeting.

"How much have you got?" shouted William.

"Five shillings," shouted the boys proudly. "I bet *you've* not got 's much as that."

"Oh, haven't we," said William, "well, where're you goin' now? It's not time for the meeting yet, is it?"

"No, there's a fair in Jenks's meadow, didn't you know?"

"No."

"Well, it's only a little one. There isn't even a proper merry-go-round. Only swings an' coconut shies an' things like that. There's jus' time to go round it before the meetin' begins."

"Come on," said William to his Outlaws, promptly forgetting everything but the fair; "we needn't spend any money there."

It was, as the boys had said, only a little fair, but the Outlaws wandered round it with great enjoyment. One item of it interested them especially. It was called the Stock Exchange machine. You put a penny in the slot and the pointer whirled round the dial. If it stopped at the name of certain commodities your penny was returned with another. If it stopped at the name of others nothing happened. As the Outlaws stood round it a man put in a penny. The finger moved round to "Coal" and twopence came back through the slot. The man pocketed it and went away. William's eyes gleamed.

"I say," he said, "that's the way to do it. We'll get

double what Douglas's aunt gave us. What'll it be?"
—he wrestled mentally with the terrific sum and finally emerged victorious—"It'll be fifteen shillings. I say, won't Victor be sold when we say we've got fifteen shillings!" He took one of the half-crowns out of his pocket. "Well, the first thing is to change this into pennies."

*   *   *   *   *

The children streamed into the Vicarage and ranged themselves on benches under the direction of the Vicar's wife. The Vicar's wife was a good woman, but she disliked children, and it was only a strong sense of duty that made her have the children's affairs at all. It was the Outlaws, of course, that she dreaded most, and, as she superintended the ranging of the children on the benches, her eyes were anxiously fixed on the doorway by which they should enter. At last they came and as soon as she saw them her heart lightened. It was quite evident that they were not in an obstreperous mood. They entered moodily, gloomily, their brows set, their eyes fixed on the floor. They took their places in the marshalled rows of their contemporaries without even scuffling. They had with them no musical instruments with which to beguile the monotony of the meeting. They forbore even to move away the chairs of their neighbours as they sat down. They sat silent, gloomy, and scowling, waiting for the missionary to enter. He entered, smiling and debonair.

"Now, children," he said, "I'll ask you in turn how much each of you have got for the Cause, and then you will come up one by one and present it to me, and I will give you a receipt for the amount with a beautiful picture that you can have framed. . . ."

"Now," he began with Victor Jameson, "how much have you got?"

Victor Jameson proudly said "seven and sixpence," and, after a few words of commendation, the missionary passed on to the next. It was at this point that William began to burrow in his pocket and to realise for the first time that he had not only lost all Douglas's aunt's money at the Stock Exchange machine, but also his own precious fourpence. The missionary had reached him now.

"And you, my little man," he said, "you were collecting in a group of four, weren't you? How much have you got?"

William's hands had just finished their search for the missing fourpence, and his gloom had changed to indignation.

He fixed a stern eye upon the missionary.

"Nothing, and you owe us fourpence," he said.

The smile dropped from the missionary's face.

"W-what?" he gasped.

"You owe us fourpence," said William. "We've tried to get a lot of money for you, but we've lost fourpence of our own on it, so you owe us fourpence."

"I don't know what you mean," said the missionary. "How much money have you actually got?"

"I've told you," said William, "nothing, and you owe us fourpence."

The Vicar's wife rose from her seat, and the Outlaws were ignominiously ejected, William still loudly protesting that the missionary owed them fourpence.

Outside the Vicarage gate William gazed at his Outlaws indignantly.

"That's the last thing I ever do for missionaries," said William, "if they don't pay their debts they can't *expect* people to help them."

The Outlaws agreed and the four of them walked gloomily down the village street. They had avoided the village street since their encounter with Mr. Theobald, but they had forgotten that in this last blow of Fate.

"I can't even get that pistol now," grumbled William, "and I don't know if I'll ever have another fourpence. I don't wonder the savages eat them."

By "them" he was referring not to pistols or four-

pences but to missionaries. "It's the same as stealin'
not payin' debts," he went on fiercely.

Then they glanced across the street.

Mr. Theobald stood in his doorway. Just over his
head the O of Theobald—staringly new and golden—
flashed in the sun.

Mr. Theobald looked at the Outlaws. He had been
feeling slightly depressed and rheumaticky, but the
sight of the Outlaws cheered him. He had completely
forgotten the trick that had been played on his sign,
but he remembered the Outlaws' offer to sell him
their hair for five pounds, and he burst into peals of
laughter remembering it.

The Outlaws looked at him.

They had completely forgotten their offer to sell
him their hair, but they remembered the glorious trick
they had played on him. Their laughter answered his
across the village street.

Mr. Theobald turned back into his shop. His de-
pression and his rheumatism had left him suddenly.
"A jolly good joke," he said to himself, "I shall see
those boys standing there and saying: 'We'll sell you
our hair for five pounds the lot,' till my dying day."

"Never mind," said William to the Outlaws as they
passed on, "what's fourpence? And the pistol'd only
get broke. And I'm jolly glad we'd not got any money
for that man. I say, whenever I think of him standing
there with THE BALD HAIRDRESSER over him, I
simply can't stop laughing."

Laughing heartily, the Outlaws passed on their way.

CHAPTER IV

THE OUTLAWS AND THE TRAMP

THE Outlaws wandered slowly down the road. It was Saturday afternoon and they were on their way to the woods with Jumble at their heels. They were discussing that subject of perennial interest—the uselessness of school.

"You never see my father sitting down to do French or any of the things he learnt to do at school," said William eloquently, "so I don't see what good it did him. Nor any of us."

"You've gotter learn to read and write, of course," said Ginger, with the air of one who wishes to be absolutely impartial. "I quite see *that*. You've gotter learn to read so as to be able to read story books, an' you've gotter learn to write so as to be able to write letters to people to thank 'em for sending you presents, 'cause if you don't they don't send any more, an' you've gotter know a bit of arithmetic so as to be able to tell if they give you wrong change in shops, but that's all. I think that when you can read and write and know enough arithmetic to know when you're getting wrong change in shops you ought to be able to leave school. That's what I think. I think all this Latin an' French an' geography's wrong. I——"

They had turned a bend in the road and there on the roadside before them sat a tramp. He was a gloriously unkempt tramp with long, red hair and a straggling, red beard. He wore the brim of an old straw hat at a jaunty angle. His coat may have first seen life at a fashionable wedding in the 'eighties. His trousers had obviously attended race meetings in their prime. His boots were tied on with string. It was clear that both the clothes and their wearer had seen better days though not in each other's company. He was cooking something over a smoky fire and singing in a deep bass voice. The Outlaws stood around him.

"Hello, my boys," he greeted them cheerfully. "Where are you off to with that fine dog?"

William's heart warmed to him. So few people perceived the fineness of Jumble at first sight like this. The first sight of Jumble—a dog of multiple pedigree —more often excited scorn and derision. William was quite accustomed to doing battle on Jumble's behalf against scoffers, as the knights of old did battle for their ladies. The "fine dog" proved the tramp a man of perspicacity and understanding.

"Can we stay and watch you?" said William.

"Come on," said the tramp genially. "Sit down and welcome, young gents. . . ."

They sat round in a semi-circle and watched the progress of the tramp's meal. He drank the steaming concoction straight from the tin. Then from a large flapping pocket he drew half a loaf and a pocket-knife and a newspaper "screw" containing cheese. Having eaten this with gusto, he drew from another part of his person a bottle whose contents he drank with even greater gusto. Then he took out a short, black clay pipe, filled it, lit it, and lay back on the path with a sigh of content, his head on his hands, gazing up at the sky.

William broke the spell-bound silence with which they had watched him.

"Can anybody be one?" he said eagerly.

"Be one what?" said the tramp.

"A tramp," said William. "We'd all like to be them."

The tramp's eyes twinkled under their bushy, red eyebrows. "It's not an easy life," he said, but he looked so carefree and merry as he said it that the Outlaws didn't believe him for a second.

"You can do jus' what you like, can't you?" said

Ginger. "Climb trees and paddle and have fights and things like that?"

"Oh, yes," said the tramp.

"And go where you like," said Douglas enthusiastically.

"And eat when you like," said Henry.

"When you've got it," agreed the tramp.

"And wear what you like," said William, gazing with admiration at the fluttering rags and the boots tied on with string.

"Oh, yes," said the tramp.

"And people aren't always making you wash and brush your hair," said Ginger, "and telling you not to get your feet wet."

"No," agreed the tramp, stroking his straggling locks. "I can't say they are."

"Well," said William earnestly, holding back Jumble, who was showing signs of dislike of their new friend, despite his opening compliment, "how do you get *in* to it? How can you *be* one?"

The tramp shook his head.

"It's not easy," he said.

"I suppose we can't till we're grown up," said William, "but what we want to know is how to get into it *then*. 'Cause I bet we all want to start the minute we're twenty-one, don't we?" he said to the others.

The others agreed—all but Jumble who uttered a dissentient growl.

"Well," said the tramp confidentially, "it's more difficult than people think. It's not generally known in fact that it's as difficult to get into as many of the other professions."

"If you've gotter pass examinations in not washin' an' in eatin' like you do," said William, "I bet we'd soon pass 'em."

The tramp shook his head.

"No, it's not that," he said, "this is one of the professions you've got to pay your way into."

The faces of the Outlaws fell. Their hands went instinctively into their empty pockets.

"Now I'll tell you all about it," said the tramp kindly, motioning them into a closer circle. They drew around, wide-eyed with eager interest. "Now it's like this," went on the tramp. "There are just a few of us at the head and we manage everything. We only admit a certain number of people to the profession each year, because, of course, it wouldn't be the grand life it is if there was too many of us." His voice sank to a sinister whisper. "People who try to set up as tramps on their own just—disappear." He uttered this word in a blood-curdling hiss and at the same time drew his finger along his throat from ear to ear. The eyes of the Outlaws started still further from their heads, and they moved yet nearer, thrilled to the core of their lawless beings.

"We've gotter be *merciless* in a profession like ours," went on the tramp, "otherwise it would go to pieces at once. Now if you young gents really want to get into it——"

The Outlaws assured him in an eager chorus that they did. "Well then, all I can say is that you're lucky to have met me. I'm the head of the whole tramp profession an' no one can get into it 'cept through me."

The Outlaws heaved deep sighs of ecstasy. Their future life seemed to stretch before them, bathed in a roseate glow. They saw themselves gloriously unwashed and unbrushed, roaming the countryside, cooking strange picnic meals on fires they had made themselves, going to bed as late as they liked, climbing trees, sleeping in barns or by the roadside.

"Now I'm goin' to do what I can for you," went on the tramp. "If I pass you into the profession, as it were, then we'll give you all our tips. We'll tell you the best places for sleeping and getting your meals. We'll tell you the places where the people'll give you food and the places where they won't, and we'll tell you the woods where you can poach safely and the woods where you can't."

Again a visible thrill of excitement passed through the Outlaws. Even Jumble showed signs of interest.

"But," went on the tramp, "there's got to be a sort of entrance fee, of course. You pay us a fee and we pass you in and hand on all our secrets to you. It's only fair, isn't it?"

The Outlaws agreed that it was, but their spirits had fallen and again their hands went to their empty pockets, hoping against hope to find some overlooked coin in them.

"How much is it?" said William anxiously.

The tramp swept a speculative glance over them, then said: "Two shillings each."

There was a sudden dejected silence. Then Ginger said hopefully:

"Well, we can't start till we're grown up and we're sure to have two shillings each when we're grown up."

The tramp shook his head sadly as if loth to curb their optimism.

"I'm afraid it's no use waiting till then," said the tramp. "You see, we've got what you might call a long waiting list. I mean, if you wait till you're grown up it will be too late. We can't have too many tramps. It would spoil the profession altogether. The only safe way of getting into it is to pay your entrance money when you're"—again his glance swept over them speculatively—"just the age you are now. Then when you're grown up and want to come on the road you'll find everything ready for you."

The Outlaws consulted together. "But we haven't got any money just now——" began William.

"*Tell* you what," interrupted the tramp good-humouredly. "I've taken a liking to you four. You're the sort we *want* on the road, see? I feel you'd be a credit to us." The Outlaws swelled visibly with pride. "I'll come back here in a week's time. Now that's a thing I've never done before. Always before I've given the candidate his chance once and for all. If he can pay his entrance fee he's in, and if he can't he'll never have a second chance. That's one of my rules. I never give anyone a second chance. But I'm going to break my rule with you. I'm going to come back here in a week's time. You'll be able to get the money by then, won't you?"

The Outlaws promised eagerly.

"Well, I'll be back in a week's time, and we'll meet here and you give me your entrance fees, and I'll give you an envelope containing an address that you must go to when you're ready to start in the profession. Now that's a thing I've never done for anyone else."

The Outlaws thanked him profusely. He held up his hand and continued impressively.

"There's only one condition," he said, "and that it that you keep this a secret between us. If any of you young gents breathe a word of this to anyone, then it's all over. You see, I don't want people to know that I've given anyone a second chance. It would be held up against me for the rest of my life. It would brand me as a weak man, which I'm not. It might even prevent me from coming to you next week with the address. So will each of you young gents give me your solemn promise not to breathe a word of this to anyone till we meet next week?"

The Outlaws promised solemnly. The tramp stowed away the remnants of his meal in his pockets, then rose, stretching himself luxuriously.

"Well," he said "this time next week we'll all meet here—you with your entrance money and me with the address. Mind you," he added, "I'm letting you off cheap. I charge most people half a crown. . . . But I like you young gents. Well—good-bye till next week."

He strolled off down the road, whistling gaily.

Jumble barked defiance at him from a safe distance The Outlaws gazed after him with rapt admiration, till he had disappeared. Then once more they drew deep breaths of ecstasy.

"Fancy *that* happenin' to *us*!" said William at last.

"I'd like to be *jus'* like him," said Ginger earnestly.

"I'm goin' to tie my boots on with string same as him," said Douglas.

"It's more *possible* than pirates or Red Indians," said Henry. "I'm glad we've chosen it."

"Two shillings each," said William meditatively, "eight shillings altogether," and, appalled by the total, added *"Gosh!"*

"We've *got* to get it," said Ginger sternly.

"Of course we have," agreed William.

"It would be awful," said Douglas, "to have to be a doctor or lawyer or something like that when we grew up just for want of two shillings now."

"How shall we get it?" said Henry. "None of my family will give me any. They say they're not going to give me any till all the things my bomb broke are paid for. Well, I didn't mean it to go off till I'd finished making it. I was jus' making it quite quietly an' suddenly it went off. Well, anyway it must have been a jolly good bomb. It wouldn't have gone off if it hadn't been. I told them that they ought to be glad because it showed how useful I'd be in time of war but they said yes, to the enemy, and things like that, and said I'd got to pay for everything it broke, and it seemed to have chosen all the most expensive things in the room to break."

But the Outlaws were tired of Henry's bomb. Though the explosion had only taken place a few days ago he had dwelt on the subject so long and so eloquently that their sympathy and interest were exhausted. After all there was nothing unique in his experience. They had all made bombs with more or less similar results.

"Let's all go and see if we can get any money at home first," said William, "an' if we can't we'll have to think of some other way of getting it. We've *got* to have it by this time next week," and added, again

"Mother, may I have some money, please?"
said William hopefully.

appalled by the magnitude of the task before them:
"*Eight* shillings! *Gosh!*"

William entered the drawing-room where his mother
sat engaged in her usual task of household mending.
She was just beginning on a sock of William's from
which the entire heel seemed to be missing.

"I wish you weren't so hard on them, dear," she
said as he entered. "Couldn't you try to walk more
lightly?"

"Uh-huh," said William vaguely, in an obliging

tone of voice, then, sitting down by her, he said hopefully: "Mother, may I have some money, please?"

"What for, dear?" said Mrs. Brown, gazing with an abstracted frown at the cavity through which both her fist and the darning "mushroom" slipped so unavailingly. "I can't think what you do to them. These were new last month."

"I only walk in them same as other people," said William, coldly, and added: "Just to spend."

"But you've got your pocket-money, dear," said Mrs. Brown.

"No I haven't," said William simply, "I've spent it. Besides, that's only twopence."

"How much do you want?" said Mrs. Brown, spanning the girth of the hole with a huge strand of wool. "I wish one could patch them."

"Two shillings," said William.

"Two *shillings*!" said Mrs. Brown indignantly. "I never *heard* of such a thing, William. Whatever do you want two shillings for?"

"It's something to do with my future," said William mysteriously.

"Nonsense!" said Mrs. Brown. "You know I don't believe in fortune telling, and two shillings is an outrageous sum to charge for it any way. You mustn't have it done."

"Have what done?"

"Your horoscope, dear, or whatever it is."

"I don't know what you mean," said William impatiently. "All I want is two shillings for a reason that you ought to be very thankful for if you knew. Because it's going to save you a lot of money."

"How is it going to save me a lot of money, dear? And I do wish you'd stand out of the light. I'm sure Robert never made holes this size. Why need you walk so *heavily*?"

"I bet I've got a bit heavier brain than Robert ever had," said William. "Naturally a brain like mine soon goes through a bit of wool."

62

"But your brain isn't in your *heel*, William."

"No, but I've got to carry the weight of it on my heel when I walk, haven't I? If you don't want to have so much darning to do," he went on hopefully, "you ought to stop me going to school. Or at any rate let me stop learning Latin. I bet it's Latin that makes my brain so heavy."

"Nonsense, William, of course you can't stop learning anything."

"Well," sighed William, "don't blame me, then, if the weight of my brain goes through a bit of wool."

He remembered the errand he had come on and began another oblique attack.

"How much money would you have to spend on me being a doctor if I wanted to be one?"

"Do you want to be a doctor, dear?" said Mrs. Brown absently. "You'll have to work much harder at school and be a lot cleaner and tidier than you are before you can be a doctor."

"I don't want to be a doctor," said William, controlling his impatience with difficulty, "but how much do you have to spend to be a doctor?"

"Several hundred pounds, I believe," said Mrs. Brown vaguely.

"Well," said William with an air of one who is about to confer a great favour. "I'm goin' to save you all that money. If you give me two shillings now you needn't spend all that money making me a doctor."

"But no one was going to make you a doctor, dear," said Mrs. Brown. "It's never even been suggested. You've never mentioned it before. I'd no idea you wanted to be a doctor."

"I *don't* want to be a doctor," said William. "Only I've got to be *something*, haven't I? I mean, whatever I am you'll have to pay money to make me it, won't you?"

"I suppose so," sighed Mrs. Brown.

"Well, what I'm tryin' to tell you," said William,

"is that I'm going to let you off all that money if you'll pay me two shillings now."

"William, what *nonsense*! You'll have to have some sort of career, I suppose, and it's sure to cost a lot of money, and you might think of that when you're so careless with your clothes, but paying two shillings now can't possibly make any difference to the money we'll have to pay for your career."

"Well, it can and it does," persisted William. "I've *got* a career already, an' two shillings'll get me into it, an' I can start straight on to it when I'm twenty-one, an' you'll never have any more trouble about me. I can't tell you all about it yet, 'cause I've promised not to, but—well," addressing the ceiling with bitter irony, "it seems a funny thing to me for a mother not even to want to pay two shillings to get her son into a career."

"Do run away, dear, and stop talking nonsense," said Mrs. Brown, exploring a second sock with a hand that again emerged into daylight through the place where William's heel had rested, "and you *will* keep standing in my light."

William went into the hall where he uttered a sarcastic laugh, then apostrophised the hat stand.

"That's the sort of mother *I've* got," he informed it. "Won't even give two shillings to get her son into a career."

The only other member of the family who was in the house was his sister, Ethel. He walked slowly up to her bedroom and knocked at the door. She said "Come in," and greeted him on his entry without enthusiasm. "Well, what do you want?"

He closed the door and went over to her window seat.

She was standing in front of her mirror, trying on a black hat. A green hat lay on her dressing-table. She took off the black hat and tried on the green one. Then she took off the green one and tried on the black one, studying her reflection the while with an anxious frown. It was obvious that she was endeavouring to decide which suited her the better.

"Ethel," said William portentously, "would you like to do something about my future?"

Ethel glanced at him still without enthusiasm.

"Yes, I would," she said grimly. "I'd like to do quite a lot about your future."

He remembered a slight misunderstanding that he had had with her the day before about a scarf that he had "borrowed" without her knowledge to use as a head band in his capacity as pirate chief. He had pointed out to her that it was not he but an enemy who had snatched it off his head and thrown it into a pond during a fight. He had pointed out that, if that had not happened, she would never even have known he had "borrowed" it, such care was he taking of it. She was still feeling annoyed about it, he supposed. Just like a girl. . . . Cunningly he approached a side of the question that might appeal to her in her present mood.

"How would you like never to see me again after I'm twenty-one, Ethel?" he said.

"It seems a long time to wait," said his sister.

He ignored the insult. "Well, if you'll give me two shillings," he said, "you'll never see me again after I'm twenty-one."

His sister was studying the effect of the green hat frowningly in the glass and didn't answer.

He repeated his offer.

"I think you're rather optimistic," she said. "Personally, I think you'll get put in prison long before you're twenty-one. By the way you go about treating other people's property as if it was yours I don't think you've got long to wait now."

"Crumbs!" he said. "I've never come across anything like the way you remember little things that no one else would ever think of again. It hasn't done it any harm. Water's *good* for things. . . . Anyway, I

65

C

wasn't talking about prison. I was talking about a career. A jolly good career that you can get me into for two shillings. Well," he ended pathetically, "that's not much for a boy's only sister to do for him, is it? Just two shillings for his career."

"It's a jolly sight more than you'll ever get out of me," she said shortly.

William sighed at this further proof of feminine heartlessness and considered his next move.

Ethel tried on the black hat again, then returned to the green one. William's eyes roved round the room. Upon the chest of drawers near the window stood the photograph of a good-looking young man in a silver frame with the name "Jimmie" scrawled across it. It was the only photograph in the room except for the photograph of Mr. and Mrs. Brown on the mantelpiece. A few weeks ago Ethel's room had been full of framed photographs of eligible youths affectionately inscribed. Ethel had been a girl of many affairs. It would be difficult indeed for a girl to have hair of the exact red-gold colour of Ethel's and eyes of the exact blue of Ethel's, and a mouth with the appealing curve of Ethel's, and not be a girl of many affairs. Young men fell in love with Ethel at first sight. They smiled on her and waited on her and swallowed her snubs with a meekness that would have amazed their families. And Ethel was kind to them or cruel to them as the whim seized her. Then quite suddenly a young man named Jimmie Moore appeared on her horizon and wrought a complete change in her. There wasn't any doubt at all that Ethel for the first time in her life was in love. And there was still less doubt that Jimmie was in love. . . .

Ethel caught sight of Jimmie now entering the garden gate, blushed, smiled, waved her hand, pulled on the green hat (she looked equally pretty in either), and started for the door. As she passed the photograph she stopped, gazed at it languishingly, then with a sudden angry movement opened the top drawer, took

66

*"If you'll give me two shillings," said William, "you'll
never see me again after I'm twenty-one."*

out an armful of the deposed photographs, flung them
scornfully into the fireplace, and departed.

William uttered his bitter laugh. "Huh," he said.
"I bet she wouldn't mind givin' *him* two shillings to
start him on a career."

He was following her out of the room when his eye
was caught by the heap of photographs in the fireplace. Photographs . . . People paid money for photographs. William didn't see very well how he could re-
duce those photographs into the cash that presumably
they represented, but it seemed a pity to leave good

saleable articles lying about to be destroyed. He gathered them up, took them into his bedroom, hid them in a drawer, and forgot all about them.

He met the Outlaws the next day. Their search for the money for their entrance fees had been as fruitless as his.

"I even asked for it for my next Christmas present," said Ginger gloomily. "Told 'em they could knock it off whatever they were goin' to buy me next Christmas an' they wouldn't . . . Well, I simply can't understand 'em. I know that if I'd got all the money they seem to have I wouldn't mind givin' two shillings to people what needed it as much as I do."

"That's what I said to 'em," said Douglas. "I said that they sent money to hospitals an' why cun't they give me a bit. I told 'em that I needed it a jolly sight more than any hospital did."

"What did they say to that?" said Henry, much impressed by the irrefutability of the argument.

"They went on and on and on about all the money they spent on my clothes an' food an' school bills. Well, I said that I'd gotter have food to keep me alive so I couldn't do without food, but I *could* do without school an' I offered to stay away from school next term jus' to save them money if they'd give me two shillings of the money they saved, which wasn't much considerin' that they pay *pounds* to send us to school, an' they wouldn't even *listen* to me . . . An' of course I couldn't tell them what it was for."

"Well," said William, "we've tried asking for it, so now we've got to try getting it other ways."

"It's no use having any sort of a show," said Ginger sadly. "We didn't make any money at all the last one we had."

"The prehistoric animal one?" said Douglas.

"Yes. Don't you remember? Only four people came an' they wouldn't pay more than a halfpenny each, an' Jumble wouldn't act a Pterodactyl properly though we'd taken *hours* teaching him how to do it, an' they all made us give them their money back. In any case," he ended gloomily, "it wouldn't have been more than twopence . . . Well, we've got to start trying to *earn* it. There's only a week."

"I'm sick of earning money," said Douglas. "You use up all your strength chopping up pounds an' *pounds* of firewood for them an' they give you a halfpenny at the end and then take it back because you've chopped up something they didn't want chopped up or because something's gone wrong with the axe. Or they promise you a halfpenny for doing an errand and then won't give it you just because the change turns out wrong or you've forgotten what they told you to get. As if one brain could hold *everything*."

"Well, anyway," said William, "we've got to *try* to earn it. And there's only a week so we've got to try jolly hard."

Gloomy but determined, the Outlaws departed to their homes.

William once more sought his mother. He meant to offer to clean her shoes for her for a week. He remembered that he had once undertaken to do this in a time of domestic crisis, and he hoped she had forgotten how he had by mistake cleaned them with the contents of a tin of fish paste that was meant for tea sandwiches that day. She had taken a great deal of trouble to get it off, but she was still followed in the village by cats whenever she wore that particular pair of shoes.

Ethel was with her mother in the drawing-room. They were discussing a bazaar. Mr. Brown had a passion for bazaars. When it wasn't the Choir Fund it was the Church Renovation Fund, and when it wasn't that it was the Nursing Fund, and when it wasn't that it was the Women's Guild. But it was always a bazaar. They took no notice of him, and he sat down gloomily to wait till he could get in with his shoe-cleaning offer.

"Mrs. Marlow's going to get Melchet's down in Hadley to stock a stall," Mrs. Brown was saying. "They give a third of whatever they make to the

Funds. We've never had that sort of thing before, but I believe it's done quite a lot, and, of course, with the Church School bazaar only just over, people really haven't a lot of things to give to this."

Something of William's gloom fell from him.

"D'you mean," he said, "that shops can sell their things at the bazaar and give a third of the money to the bazaar and keep the rest?"

"It's done quite a lot now, dear," said Mrs. Brown absently. "I don't like it."

A light broke through William's countenance.

"D'you mean," he said, "that *anyone* could sell things there an' give the bazaar a third of the money an' keep the rest themselves."

"I suppose so," said Mrs. Brown still absently, "if they'd got anything that anyone would want to buy."

Then she seemed suddenly to awake to the fact of William's presence. "What do you want, dear?" she said.

"Nothing, thanks," said William as he disappeared through the doorway.

His Outlaws did not entirely share his optimism.

"But we've got nothing to *sell*," objected Henry. "You can't get money for *nothing*."

"We've got to *make* something to sell," said William sternly. "There's four whole days. Surely we can *make* somethin' in four days."

"Yes, but *what*?" demanded the Outlaws.

"*Tell* you what!" said William, as another bright idea struck him, "let's have it a sort of second-hand stall—what they call a White Elephant Stall." He uttered the words with contempt, remembering the acute disappointment he had suffered on first seeing the contents of the stall so misleadingly named. "Well, surely we can all find some old things we don't want."

"Yes," objected Douglas, "but most of the things I don't want no one else'd want either."

"Oh, do shut up," said William wearily. "If the great men in history had all gone on like you there

70

wouldn't have been any great deeds done. We've got to get a stall full of things that we don't want ourselves but that other people pay lots of money for. An' we've got to have eight shillings left over when we've paid a third to the bazaar."

Even Ginger shook his head sadly at this. He knew by experience that there were times when William's optimism ran away with him.

And the result of their endeavour, as viewed in the old barn on the morning of the Sale of Work, was not encouraging.

Henry had brought a rather unsavoury pail, with half the bottom out, that he had come upon in a ditch. He said vaguely that somebody might find it useful for something.

Douglas had brought an old prayer book from which the entire Morning Service and half the Evening Service was missing, and a pair of socks that his mother had thrown away as undarnable.

Ginger had brought a bird's nest and a dead fern in a pot, which he had tied to a stick in order to keep it in an upright position, and labelled: "Rare brown Furn from the Troppiks."

William's contribution was a teapot without a spout, a razor of Robert's that had lost its blade, and a newt in a jam jar.

They gazed at the collection dispassionately.

"Well, we're not likely to get eight shillings for those," said Henry, who had spent the evening of the previous day working out the sum.

"We're likely to get a lot for that rotten old bucket you've brought," said William. "Why didn't you take a little *trouble*?"

There followed an acrimonious discussion on the rival merits of the white elephants, which was finally ended by William who said:

"Well, *talkin'* won't get us the eight shillings. I vote we all go home again and see if we can find something else."

So they all went home again to see if they could find something else. William went up to his bedroom and looked around it without much hope.

If he took any of his personal belongings, such as his soap dish or hair brush, they would be recognised and indignantly reclaimed by his mother. He opened his drawers one after the other—collars, ties, stockings. He couldn't possibly take any of them. His mother would recognise them at once. He opened the long drawer at the bottom. Ethel's photographs. He had quite forgotten them. He looked at them doubtfully. He remembered the zest with which his mother treasured all her family photographs. These men's mothers or aunts might be at the bazaar and might want to buy their photographs. It was worth trying. He gathered them together and set off briskly again to the old barn.

*   *   *   *   *

There was a strange undercurrent of excitement in the crowded room that seemed to centre in the younger set.

Dolly Clavis, a comely damsel of about eighteen, was making her way tempestuously to the door. Her head was held high, her eyes were flashing angrily, her lips set in a haughty line. Beside her, pale and distraught, strode George (Douglas's brother). He was running his hands through his hair, then throwing them out in passionate protest.

"I tell you it's all a mistake," he said. "I never admired her. Never."

"Oh no, never," shrilled the outraged damsel sarcastically, "and there's your photograph standing for the whole world to see with 'To Ethel from her most humble and faithful admirer, George.' 'Her most humble and faithful admirer, George'!" she repeated furiously.

"I tell you it isn't me," pleaded the unhappy youth. "I tell you it's someone else who happens to have my

72

name and a face like mine. I tell you I hate and despise Ethel Brown. It was *months* ago and I never knew she'd kept that photograph. I don't know how the hateful little wretch got hold of it. I tell you——"

"I won't listen to a word you have to say," said the lady. "Not a *word*. I'll never speak to you again. Never. Going round giving your photographs to Ethel Brown with stuff you ought to be ashamed of written all over them, and then pretending you love me!"

"I do love you," protested the youth wildly. "It was *months* ago, and I didn't mean it even at the time, and it was before I got to know you, and I tell you I hate Ethel Brown and——"

"I never want to see you or hear of you again," repeated the damsel, keeping however carefully within sight and earshot. "Go away. I hate you."

"Listen!" pleaded the youth. "Just listen——"

They had reached the door of the room. Another youth and damsel were entering it—happy, carefree, smiling fondly at each other.

The youth was Hector—Ginger's brother and George's friend. The maiden was a local belle of the name of Peggy Barton.

As the couples passed each other, George just had time to pull his friend aside and whisper wildly:

"Go and buy your photograph. Quick. There—over there by the door. Don't let her see."

Then he passed on with his offended lady love, explaining, exhorting, beseeching.

Hector gazed after them, his mouth hanging open with amazement.

"What did he say?" said Peggy.

Hector pulled himself together. "I—I don't know," he said. He was bewildered but uneasy. There had been urgent secrecy in George's whisper. There had been something disquieting in its tragic intensity.

He made his way over into the corner indicated by George. It was rather a crowded corner, rather a hilarious corner. He pushed his way through the

73

crowd. There behind a stall made by two packing-cases joined together stood William, Ginger, Douglas and Henry. On the packing-cases was ranged a heterogeneous assortment of rubbish and in the front of it a row of photographs and next to them a card bearing the legend: "Fotografs—1d. eech."

As a matter of fact Hector did not realise that there was a row of photographs. All he saw was his own photograph. It was hideously large, hideously lifelike. It seemed to fill the whole room. It was inscribed in mountainous letters of startling blackness with the words: "To Ethel, the most beautiful Girl in the World, from her faithful Hector." The words seemed not to be merely inscribed on the photograph. They seemed to detach themselves from it and go shouting about the room. He turned and plunged back, panic stricken, through the crowd.

"What was there?" said Peggy. "Why didn't you go to see?"

"I did see," said Hector smiling a ghastly smile and mopping his brow. "There wasn't anything. I swear there wasn't anything."

"What are people laughing at then?" said Peggy. "I'm going to see."

"No, don't!" said Hector wildly, "don't!"

"What on earth's the matter?" said the bewildered Peggy. "I *am* going to see."

"You mustn't," implored Hector. "Honestly you mustn't. You—you simply mustn't."

"If it's something improper," said Peggy primly, "I think it ought to be reported to the Vicar."

"It isn't anything improper," said Hector. "I swear it isn't."

"Well, I'm going to see what it is," said Peggy, plunging through the crowd. There was only one thing to be done and Hector did it. He plunged in before her, took out the first coin his fingers came upon (it happened to be a shilling), flung it at William, seized his photograph, crumpled it up, and thrust it into his pocket. When Peggy came he was standing by the packing-cases, gazing down at the photographs.

"Well," he said breathlessly but with rather a good attempt at nonchalance, "I told you there was nothing."

She gazed at the photographs, first with amazement then with suspicion (she was making sure that Hector's wasn't among them), then with aloof disdain.

"Why on *earth* did you want me to come and look at this?" she said coldly.

"I didn't," he said simply.

"I think it's in horribly bad taste," she said, turning away with a haughty shrug.

"So do I," said Hector, venturing to take her arm to pilot her back through the crowd.

She allowed the piloting in a way that was distinctly encouraging.

"I simply can't see what people find so attractive in Ethel Brown," she said.

Hector dug the crumpled photograph more deeply into his pocket, and skilfully intensified his activities as pilot.

"Neither do I," he said, "I never have done."

The Outlaws were surprised and bewildered by the effect of their White Elephant stall. The laughter of the bystanders at the beginning was unexpected, but grown-up laughter generally was unexpected, and the Outlaws had learnt to ignore it. The sudden appearance of Dolly Clavis, however, engaged in angry denunciation of Ginger's brother, who was escorting her, was thrilling and quite inexplicable. She pointed with eloquent gestures to the White Elephant Stall and asked George passionately why he hadn't told her from the beginning that he loved another and was only playing with her. The Outlaws concluded that she had suddenly gone mad. It seemed the only possible explanation. They were still more surprised when Hector pushed his way to the stall and with an expression of frozen horror on his face flung a shilling at them, seized his photograph and disappeared. Very thoughtfully William took his notice and altered one penny to one shilling. Evidently the market value of old photographs was higher than he had supposed.

In the distance he saw Hector stop and whisper to Jameson Jameson who was escorting Marion Dexter, another youthful belle. The smile dropped from Jameson Jameson's face like something being wiped off a slate, and, as if galvanised suddenly by some electric shock, he shot through the crowd to the Outlaws' stall, leaving his attendant nymph gazing around with bewilderment. Baring his teeth in fury at the Outlaws he flung them the first coin his fingers found in his pocket (a two-shilling piece), seized his photograph and tore it up, thrust the pieces into his pocket and shot back to the bewildered Marion. William could see him in the distance smiling a fixed and ghastly smile as he explained to her that he thought he saw someone fainting and had gone to see if he could help.

The next surprise for the Outlaws was provided by Glory Tomkins, a damsel of about nineteen. She strolled up to the White Elephant Stall and gazed at it, smiling a smile of superior amusement. Suddenly her eyes fell upon the photograph of Marmaduke Morency inscribed with the words: "To Ethel the Only Girl in the World for Marmaduke." It so happened that on Glory's mantelpiece at home stood an identical photograph with an identical inscription except that for 'Ethel' was substituted the name 'Glory.' Glory's blue eyes bulged, her rosebud mouth opened wide, then tightened ominously. She gave a low cry of rage, turned on her heel and set out in quest of Marmaduke. She found him looking for her, an innocent smile on his lips, regardless of his doom.

She seized him by the arm and drew him to the White Elephant Stall. She pointed to his photograph with a gesture eloquent of anger, scorn and grief. He seized it and tore it up, ignoring the notice that

76

advertised its price. She had turned on her heel and departed, but not too quickly. He caught her up before she reached the door. It took three hours, four boxes of chocolates from the Confectionery Stall, a large bunch of expensive flowers from the Flower Stall, a bottle of scent from the Fancy Stall, to convince her that he had never really loved Ethel and that she was to him the only girl in the world. And even then she continued to refer to the matter. News of the stall spread swiftly and urgently among the youthful males of the neighbourhood, most of whom had passed through the Ethel stage of calf love. They came in a furtive stream to the White Elephant Stall to buy back their photographs, exhibiting signs of scorn and anger, but obviously nervous and never waiting for change. It was perhaps a good thing that Ethel had decided to play truant from the Sale of Work, and go for a walk with Jimmie Moore, intending just to look in on it on her way home.

It wasn't till the last photograph had been sold that Authority suddenly realised that there was an unauthorised entertainment going on in the room. Authority had till now been so busy at the Produce Stall and the Household Stall and the Toilet Stall and the Fancy Stall and the Flower Stall and the Confectionery Stall, and the crowd was so thick around these stalls, that it was not at first officially noticed that the crowd was thicker in one withdrawn corner of the room than anywhere else. Nor was Authority aware of the excitement that spread like wildfire among the young beaux of the neighbourhood. Authority of course had never given its photograph to Ethel. It had contented itself with finding occasion for conversation with her and lending her the novels of Dickens and Sir Walter Scott. But Authority, mounting upon a ladder in order to restore the symmetry of the festooning of the Fancy Stall (the drawing-pins that were supposed to hold it up having responded to the force of gravity), and casting a commanding eye round the room, spied the four Outlaws behind their two packing-cases of White Elephants. Authority hastily descended from the ladder in order to investigate the situation. The crowd melted away to let Authority pass. The last of the photographs had just been sold. A pale and distraught youth was scattering its fragments to the winds of heaven and swearing never again to commit his features to memory on photographic plate. His inamorata, who by an unkind stroke of fate had found her way to the White Elephant Stall before him, had gone home after an outburst of inspired invective in which she had told him that he was a heartless brute, that she had hated him from the moment she first set eyes on him, that he had cast her aside like an old glove, and that he could *have* Ethel Brown. He had no doubt at all of being able ultimately to melt her, but he knew by experience that it would be a long and expensive process.

Authority found the four Outlaws entrenched behind two packing-cases containing an old pail, a ragged prayer book, a bird's nest, an old pair of socks, a broken teapot, a dead fern, a bladeless razor and a newt, waiting hopefully for purchasers. After all, as William said, if people would buy old photographs there wasn't any reason why they shouldn't buy old pails and prayer books and socks.

"What's all this?" said Authority severely.

"It's a White Elephant Stall," explained William coldly, "if you want to buy anything, you can buy it, and if you don't you'd better go away and stop taking up room."

"Who gave you permission to have this stall?" said Authority, looking with stern contempt at their not very impressive array of White Elephants.

"No one," said William. "Anyone can have a stall if they give one third of the money to the Bazaar."

"I never heard such nonsense," said Authority. "Clear out at once."

William looked for a moment as if about to dispute

this order, then realised that he was growing very bored with his White Elephant Stall, and that on the whole, thanks to the boom in second-hand photographs, it had done as well as was necessary. With slow dignity he collected the remains of his white elephants and departed with his Outlaws. Outside the building they counted their money. It exceeded their wildest hopes.

"Crumbs!" said William. "It'll pay our entrance fees and *more*! And all with old photographs!"

They counted out a third of it, and William took it to his mother, who was at the Fancy Stall engaged in trying to persuade an old lady who had no telephone to buy a telephone cover.

"What's that, dear?" she said absently, when William poured a little heap of coins into her hand.

"It's a third," said William.

"A what, dear?" she said.

"A third," repeated William. "A third of our stall."

"What stall, dear?" said Mrs. Brown.

"White Elephant Stall," said William.

"But you hadn't got a White Elephant Stall," said Mrs. Brown.

"Yes, we had," said William, "and that's a third."

"William," said Mrs. Brown vaguely apprehensive, "you haven't been in any mischief, have you?"

"Me," said William indignantly, "of course not."

Mrs. Brown had no time to investigate further. The old lady was obviously beginning to doubt the usefulness of a telephone cover to a telephoneless household. Mrs. Brown poured William's coins into the cash box, hoping that it was all right, and turned to the old lady.

"It would make," she said, "a very pretty tea cosy with only a very little alteration. Or," vaguely, "you could keep things in it."

As William passed out of the room he met Ethel and Jimmie Moore just coming into it.

The Outlaws, in a state of eager excitement, stood at the point of the road at which they had met the tramp. Each held his two shillings in his hand. Their eyes were fixed on the point at which the gaily swaggering figure with its fluttering rags should appear.

"S'pose he doesn't come," said Ginger.

"I *bet* he'll come," said William.

"I'm going to start the *day* I'm twenty-one," said Douglas.

"Will they give us old clothes?" said Henry. "Or shall we just have to wait till ours get old?"

"I'm goin' to have a hat just like his without a top," said William.

"And eat bread and cheese with an old pen-knife," added Ginger with a blissful smile.

"And go about in woods and fields all day without having to keep tidy and come home to meals."

"And stay up as long as you like and no one bothering how dirty you get."

"He's a bit late," said Douglas anxiously.

"Well, he's a sort of King of the tramps," said Henry. "I expect he's jolly busy. Prob'ly they've got some sort of a Parliament on, and he's got to open it or something."

At that moment the gaily swaggering figure appeared at the end of the road and waved to them in friendly greeting. They ran towards it excitedly. There was a pleased smile on the gentleman's sandy countenance. He had evidently not been quite sure of finding them there.

"Well this is splendid," he said. "Got your money?"

"Yes," said William making himself the spokesman. "Yes. We've got the money all right. Have you got the address?"

With impressive dignity the sandy gentleman took a grimy envelope out of his pocket.

"You must promise," he said, "not to open this till three minutes after I've gone and," he added still more impressively, "you must never show anyone what's inside it."

Thrilling from head to foot with excitement, the Outlaws promised.

"Well, now let's have your money," said the sandy gentleman. His eyes were glistening thirstily. "Half a crown each, wasn't it?"

"No, two shillings," said William.

"Oh yes, I forgot. Two shillings."

The Outlaws held out grimy hands in each of which reposed two very warm shillings.

But just as they did so something else happened. Round the bend in the road came a policeman, and, the minute he appeared, the tramp seemed suddenly and miraculously to vanish. They saw him for a second in the distance, his rags fluttering in the wind. A moment later he had completely disappeared.

The policeman, who was rather stout, pursued him for a short distance conscientiously if ineffectively, then returned to the Outlaws, mopping his brow.

"Tryin' to get money out of you, was he?" he said.

"We were paying him our entrance fee," said William with dignity.

"Trust him to get money out of anyone," said the policeman. "Soon as I saw him round here I knew he was up to no good."

"Do you know him?" said William.

"Should think I do," said the policeman. "We all know Sandy Dick. He's got money out of police headquarters pretending to be a Scotland Yard man on a job. He's got money out of a bishop pretending to be a converted cannibal. He can get money out of *anyone*. I suppose he was getting it out of you?"

"He's left the address anyway," said William picking up the envelope which the tramp had dropped at the policeman's appearance.

Eagerly he tore it open. There was nothing inside it.

"What did you think there'd be inside?" said the policeman.

They told him the whole story.

He put back his head and roared with laughter. With the roars of his laughter eddying around them, the Outlaws tried to see the affair as they had seen it a few minutes ago—tried and failed. The flight of their "chief," the empty envelope, the policeman's raucous and rather tactless merriment, stripped the exploit of its glamour and revealed them to themselves as inglorious dupes. But, inglorious as the affair might be, it had its redeeming features. It would have been much worse if the policeman had appeared after they had yielded up their "entrance fee," instead of just before.

They looked at their combined eight shillings with rising spirits.

"Well, my lads," said the policeman with a grin, "you'll be wiser next time."

"You're not going to put him in prison, are you?" said Henry rather anxiously.

" 'Im?" said the policeman. "Sandy Dick? 'E'll be at Newcastle by now. You never knew such a sprinter. By the time you think you've got him nicely copped in Land's End you suddenly find 'e's in John o' Groats. That's the sort of chap *e* is. You should see 'im play the toff too when 'e likes. Pass as a duke any day, 'e could."

The spirits of the Outlaws rose still higher. They had been duped by no common rogue. It was, after all, rather an honour to have been taken in by Sandy Dick.

The policeman had adjusted his helmet and belt and set off down the road.

The Outlaws stood and surveyed the wealth that was left so unexpectedly on their hands.

"Come on," said William, "I'm jolly hungry. Let's go'n' buy some lemonade and cream blodges."

The Outlaws walked down to the village with a carefree nonchalant swagger that was partly a copy of Sandy Dick's and partly expressive of their feelings.

Eight shillings are eight shillings, and a feast of lemonade and cream blodges in the hand is after all worth any amount of glorious careers in the bush.

*   *   *   *   *

In the woods Ethel walked with her chosen swain. "Jimmie," she said thoughtfully, "do you remember the sale of work yesterday?"

"Yes, darling," said Jimmie.

"Well, didn't you notice," said Ethel still more thoughtfully, "that people looked at me in a *funny* way?"

"What sort of a funny way?" said Jimmie.

"I don't know. Just a *funny* way."

"What sort of people?"

"Oh, George and Hector and Jameson and Marmaduke and people like that."

"I didn't notice," said Jimmie, "but I'll go and push all their faces in for them if you like. No trouble at all. I'd enjoy doing it."

"Oh no," said Ethel, "it wasn't that sort of a look. It was—well, I simply can't describe it. It was just *funny*."

"Well don't talk about them," said Jimmie, "it's a waste of breath. Let's forget them and talk about ourselves."

So they forgot them and talked about themselves.

*   *   *   *   *

The Outlaws sat round the marble-topped table in the village confectioner's. At each place was a glass of lemonade and in the middle of the table a large dish (already twice replenished) of cream blodges.

It was not often that the Outlaws could feast off such dainties *ad nauseam*. To-day they could. It was a strange and glorious feeling to be able to eat cream blodge after cream blodge without having to keep an anxious eye on the penny that each represented. The Outlaws did not in fact remember ever having had such riches at their disposal before.

"We can buy some new fishing nets after this," said Ginger. "Ours are full of holes."

"And some more marbles," said Douglas.

"And *lots* of sweets," said Henry.

"You know I never thought we'd make half so much money by the White Elephant Stall," said William.

"It was the photographs that people paid so much for," said Ginger.

"Yes," said Douglas, "and the funny thing was they all bought their own photographs. I thought it would be their mothers or aunts who'd buy them."

"Yes, I thought it was jolly conceited of them," said William, "they seemed jolly bad tempered about it, too. It was all," he said reflectively, "a bit queer, somehow."

"Yes, but it's been all right for us," said Ginger.

The Outlaws dismissed the slightly puzzling element that there had undoubtedly been about the affair, and, ordering another dish of cream blodges and four more bottles of lemonade, surrendered themselves to the cheering reflection that it had been all right for them.

CHAPTER V

WILLIAM AND THE SLEEPING MAJOR

THE Outlaws were wandering through the wood, discussing what to do with the afternoon that, full of glorious possibilities, lay before them.

"Let's try'n' make up some game we've never played before," said Ginger.

"Yes," said Henry. "Let's——"

He stopped.

They had reached a bend in the path and there, just in front of them, by the side of the path, was an elderly man of military appearance who was fast asleep in a bath chair with the remains of a picnic around him.

At first the Outlaws approached very carefully, lest any unguarded movement should rouse the sleeping warrior to wakefulness and wrath. Gradually, however, they grew bolder, and began to approach with less caution. Finally they stood round his chair. He had not even stirred in his sleep.

"He's dead," said Ginger cheerfully.

"He can't be," said Douglas. "He's breathin'."

"P'raps he's dyin'," said Ginger still more cheerfully. "P'raps if we wait a bit, he'll stop breathin'."

They stood round the bath chair, watching and waiting expectantly, but the deep breathing still continued.

"He's not dyin'," said Ginger, disappointedly.

William cleared his voice and said, "Hi!" in a voice only slightly louder than Ginger's.

At this moment a wasp stung Douglas, and he uttered a loud yell. The Outlaws turned and fled precipitately from the scene. When they had fled for some distance, however, it occurred to them that they were not being pursued. They stopped and looked back. The elderly gentleman was still slumbering peacefully in his bath chair. Very cautiously, in fear of a ruse, they returned. But there was no ruse. The elderly gentleman continued to slumber peacefully. They gathered round him again, and began to make noises of various degrees of audibility, to see whether the sleeping occupant of the bath chair would show any reaction to any of them. He continued to slumber peacefully. They grew bolder.

"Boo!"

"Yah!"

"*Hoi!*"

"Bah!"

There was a certain thrill about the proceeding. It was like baiting a lion in his den. At any minute the ferocious old gentleman might suddenly awaken and leap on them in fury. But he didn't, and at last they tired of it.

"Come on!" said Henry. "Let's go'n' play at something."

"Let's see what he's been havin'," said Ginger.

Search in the picnic basket revealed the remainder of a pork pie, and several buns, and a small empty bottle that had contained wine.

"Seems sort of waste to leave this," said William, holding up the pork pie. "It'll only get stale an' he can't eat anythin' dyin' like this. People're always tellin' us that it's wrong to leave bits of food lyin' about in woods after picnics an' such-like. I bet it'd be a kindness to eat it jus' to clear it out of the way. Well, we don't want the pore ole man to get into trouble for it anyway."

"He won't if he dies," objected Ginger.

"Oh, shut up arguin' about it," said William, taking a large bite out of the meat pie and handing it to Douglas.

For the next few minutes the Outlaws were deprived of the power of speech. It was a largish piece of meat pie, and provided them with three bites each. The custom of the Outlaws when sharing anything in the nature of a pork pie was to take a bite in turns till the thing was finished. By dint of long practice, their mouths had acquired the knack of accommodating, as a "bite," a portion of the whole that would have staggered an ordinary adult. Occasionally, of course, one of them overreached himself. The mouth had to be able to close completely over the mouthful or it did not count and the next turn had to be missed. The consumption of the meat pie and cakes occupied them for the next few minutes. Then Ginger approached the sleeping warrior.

"He's not dead yet," he announced, speaking in a muffled voice. "He's still breathin'."

"I don' think he's goin' to die," said Douglas. "I don' think he'd look as red as that. Not if he was goin' to die. He'd look pale. Dyin' people always look pale."

"Oh, well," said William, who was losing interest in the question, "p'raps he isn't. It's jus' possible that he isn't. He may've got some sort of illness where you go on sleepin' for the rest of your life an' never wake up. I've heard of illnesses like that. You go on sleepin' for the rest of your life an' never wake up."

"I bet I wouldn't mind an illness like that," said Ginger wistfully. "You'd never have to go to school or church or anythin'. Better than the sort of illnesses I always get. Mumps," he ended bitterly. "Mumps, and earaches an' things like that."

"Oh, come on," said Douglas. "Let's go and play at somethin'."

"Yes, let's," said Henry, "this is a trespass wood, too. You know how mad they were last time they found us in it. Let's get out of it quick."

"Well, *he's* not got no right to be in it either," said William, who was obviously unwilling to abandon his find. "I don' think we ought to leave him in here where he's got no right any more than we have. We oughtn't to leave a pore ole man like this to be gone on at by that keeper the way he goes on at us. Well, I'm not goin' to go away an' leave him. I'm going to take him along with me."

The Outlaws made no serious objection. To the other three as to William it seemed rather tame to go away, leaving their strange and intriguing find behind them.

It was a breathless moment when William laid his hands upon the handle of the bath chair, and began cautiously to propel it along the path. His tongue was extended to its full length in the stress of the moment, his eyes were fixed warily upon the nodding head, his whole body poised for flight. But the breathless moment passed. The nodding head continued to nod. The eyes in the fiery face remained closed. The band began to breathe freely again, began even to raise their voices as they discussed the situation together.

"If he died sudden now," said Ginger importantly, "there'd be a ninquest an' we'd have to go to it."

"What's a ninquest?" said William suspiciously.

"Whenever anyone dies sudden," said Ginger, "they have a ninquest to find out why they're dead, and the ones that were with them when they died have to go to it. And then if anyone's killed him they catch 'em that way. He has to go to it an' so they catch him there."

"I say," said William excitedly, pointing to his cargo, "let's have a ninquest on him."

"We can't," said Henry. "He's still breathin'."

"That doesn't matter," said William impatiently; "we can pretend he's dead, can't we? He's as near dead as anyone could be—not movin' an' with his eyes closed. The only difference is that he's breathin' an' that's not much. Yes, let's have a ninquest on him. I'll be the judge."

"It isn't a judge when it's a ninquest," said Ginger importantly.

"What is it, then?" challenged William.

Ginger, frowning deeply, pursued an elusive word in his mind for a minute before replying.

"It's a—a coronationer."

"A what?" said William.

"A coronationer," said Ginger a little more firmly, seeing that William was merely challenging his statement for form's sake and not at all because he disbelieved it.

"I knew he was," said William. "I was only seein' if you knew. Well, I'll be the coronationer an' you can be the murderer, an' Douglas can be the policeman an' Henry can be——" He appealed to Ginger, who had by this time established his reputation as an authority on inquests. "Who else has there got to be besides a coronationer an' a murderer an' a policeman?"

"There's always gotter be a doctor at a ninquest," said Ginger.

"All right, Henry can be the doctor," said William.

The difficulties of getting the bath chair over the stile into the field where the old barn was, proved insuperable, and so the inquest was held in a part of the road just near the stile. Fortunately it was a little-used road, so the band could conduct operations without fear of interruption. William, as coroner, sat on the fence with the sleeping warrior in the bath chair, as corpse, just in front of him. The murderer and policeman and doctor grouped themselves around the corpse. The coroner opened proceedings by saying, "Ladies and gentlemen——" then, further invention failing him, pointed to the corpse and addressed the doctor.

"Is this man dead?"

"I should think you could see for yourself he is," said the doctor; "use your eyes, can't you?"

"You jolly well shut up talking to me like that," said the coroner indignantly, "and you ought to say 'Sir' or 'My lord' or something like that when you speak to me. And it's *your* business knowin' when people are dead, not mine. If you're a doctor you're supposed to have passed examinations in tellin' whether people are dead."

The doctor conducted a lengthy and elaborate examination of the corpse, keeping a careful distance from it.

"Yes," he pronounced, at last, "he's dead all right."

"What did he die of?" said the coroner.

The doctor conducted another examination—yet more lengthy and elaborate—keeping a still more careful distance from it.

"He's died of slow poison," he pronounced at last.

"Who poisoned him?" said the coroner.

"I did," said the murderer.

"What for?" said the coroner.

" 'Cause I wanted to," said the murderer.

"All right. You'll have to be hung," said the coroner.

"I don't care," said the murderer.

The coroner turned to the policeman.

"You go an' hang him an' mind you do it properly, or you'll get hung yourself as well."

They proceeded to hang Ginger, who made a most satisfactorily recalcitrant criminal. He escaped twice, and struggled so realistically that the doctor retired from the fight half-way through to nurse a black eye, and the coroner was sent flying into a ditch.

Finally Ginger himself tired of it and allowed himself to be hanged, indulging in such realistic death struggles that William almost regretted not having chosen that rôle himself. They then returned to the gentleman in the bath chair, who was still sound asleep. William had the brilliant idea of taking a letter, which protruded slightly out of a pocket, in order to find out his name. The letter was addressed to Major Franklin.

"That's his name," explained William. "Well, I'm gettin' a bit tired of this game. I vote we go'n play Red Indians for a bit."

The others were inclined to receive this proposal favourably, but Ginger pointed to the man in the bath chair, and said: "Yes, but what about *him*? We can't jus' leave him here."

"Why not?" said William.

"Well, s'pose a motor-cycle or somethin' like that comes along an' kills him? They'll say it was our fault for leavin' him here."

At that moment Victor Jameson passed along the road with a small train of followers. Victor Jameson and the Outlaws were on friendly terms.

"I say," said William, pointing to the sleeping warrior, "would you like him?"

Victor Jameson looked at the sleeping warrior with interest.

"Who is he?" he asked.

"Dunno," said William, "but you can have him for sixpence. You can have him, chair an' all, for sixpence. It's jolly cheap."

"Who does he belong to?" said Victor.

"He belongs to us," said William; "we found him in a wood."

"Why is he asleep like that?"

"Dunno. But he's all right. He's jolly fine to play games with. He goes on sleepin' like this an' he never wakes up. Look here, you can have him *an'* his chair for fivepence halfpenny. It's a bargain."

Victor and his followers submitted the bargain to a lengthy inspection, and consulted together.

"You can pretend he's a king on a throne or someone's ole grandfather," said William. "Or if you're playin' pirates, he'd do for the ship you're attackin' or anything like that. An' he never wakes up." He paused, then said: "Fourpence halfpenny, then. It's jolly cheap."

"We'll take him," Victor finally announced to William, "if you'll let us have him for threepence."

"All right," said William, "threepence."

They handed over the threepence, and the Outlaws departed.

*   *   *   *   *

A girl and a young man stood in the clearing in the wood and looked about them desperately.

"But—but we left him here," said the girl wildly, "we left him here after lunch, he *can't* have gone away."

The young man took out his handkerchief and mopped his brow.

"What—what a ghastly thing to have happened!" he said.

"Well, *do* something about it, can't you?" snapped the girl.

"What *can* I do?" retorted the youth with spirit.

"Find him."

"I'm going to. But we've got to think out some plan of action first. I mean before we start looking for him we've got to form some sort of idea where he is, haven't we?"

"Well, where can he be?"

"I don't know. That's what we've got to try and think of."

"One of the keepers can't have turned him out of the wood, can they?"

"Of course not. They all knew that we've got permission to come in."

"He—Charlie, he can't have wakened up and found we'd gone off and left him, can he?"

"I don't see how he can."

"You—you put the sleeping-draught in his wine, didn't you?"

"Yes. It's always acted before."

"Oh, dear," moaned the girl. "It's a judgment on us. It was wrong."

"Nonsense. You know what he's like when he doesn't have it. Keeps us dancing attendance on him all the afternoon, and his temper absolutely foul. Now if I put a drop of sleeping-draught into his wine he sleeps like a lamb and wakes up as fresh as a daisy."

"Charlie, he's been kidnapped and they're holding him up to ransom!"

"Rats!"

"He'll be mad if he finds that we go off and leave him, you know. He thinks that we spend all the afternoon sitting by his bath chair and reading and waiting for him to wake up for tea."

"Well, let's go down to the village and see if we can find any news of him there."

"Yes, that seems the best thing to do."

They went down to the village and the first person they met was William.

The Outlaws had had a most enjoyable game of Red Indians and had just separated to go home for tea.

"Excuse me, little boy," said the girl sweetly, "but have you seen anything of an old gentleman in a bath chair?"

William considered. So recent and vivid was his memory of the game of Red Indians that it was some time before the memory of the old gentleman in the bath chair came to him through the mists of the past. A guarded look spread over his face as the memory returned.

"Why?" he said. "Have you lost one?"

"Yes," said the girl eagerly. "My cousin and I took our uncle into the wood for a little picnic and left him there just a minute after lunch—well, not much longer than a minute, anyway—and when we came back he'd gone."

"Oh," said William, assuming an expression of surprise and concern as a cloak to the quick and anxious cogitations that were taking place in his mind. "Have —have you looked for him in the wood?"

"Yes," said the girl, "at least we looked just near the place we left him. It was one of his gouty days, you see. He couldn't walk any distance at all. Have —have you seen anything of an old gentleman in a bath chair?"

The young lady had blue eyes and a winning manner and William was anxious to help her, but it was a situation requiring delicate handling. He assumed the expression of one who is thinking deeply, and then of one to whom some distant but illuminating memory has just returned. Both expressions were quite well done.

"Wait a minute," he said, "I think I remember a boy tellin' me he'd seen an ole gentleman in a bath chair."

"Oh, do tell us where he lives," said the girl, "and we'll go and ask him."

"No, I'll ask him," said William kindly, "don' you bother askin' him. I know him, you see, an' so I'd better ask him. He might remember it better with me askin' him."

"It's most *awfully* kind of you," said the girl gratefully.

"Oh, that's quite all right," said William, "that's quite all right. I like helpin' people."

He led them down the road to Victor Jameson's house and looked anxiously about. There were no signs of the old gentleman in his bath chair.

"You'd better stay out here in the road," he said to the man and girl, " 'cause—'cause," with a sudden flash of inspiration, " 'cause they've got a very savage dog. It knows me, but anyone it doesn't know it goes for something terrible."

His new friends seemed impressed by this argument. He hoped they would catch no glimpse of the friendly puppy who was the Jamesons' sole canine staff. They stood in the road outside the gate while he made his cautious way round to the back of the house. There he uttered the low whistle which took the place of his visiting-card. All his friends and acquaintances knew it. At once Victor emerged (also cautiously, for visits from William were not encouraged by his parents) from the side door.

"I say," said William in a hoarse whisper, "where's that ole man we sold you? They're lookin' for him. I'll buy him back for twopence. You've had him all the afternoon an' you can't expect to get as much for him as you paid for him after havin' him all afternoon."

"We've not got him," said Victor, "we played with him for a bit an' then we got tired of him—you can't play many games with him, you know—so we sold him to the Badlow twins. They wanted him for a tunnel to their train. They've got a new train an' they wanted to make it go under his chair for a tunnel so we said they couldn't 'less they bought him, so they bought him."

"How much did they pay for him?" said William.

"Twopence."

"All right," said William, "I'll go an' buy him back off them an' they'll have to take a penny for him. They can't have more than a penny for him if they only paid twopence an've had him all afternoon."

He returned slowly and thoughtfully to the waiting couple. The girl was standing at a safe distance from the gate, watching it fearfully, obviously prepared every moment for the sally of a ferocious hound.

"This," said William, fixing them both with his most expressionless regard, "this isn't the *acshul* boy what saw him. He says that what he meant wasn't that he'd *acshully* seen him but that he'd seen someone what'd said he'd seen him."

"Did he tell you who it was?" said the girl.

"Yes," said William, "I'll go with you to him now."

"It's really very kind of you," said the young man gratefully.

"Oh, no," said William. "It's quite all right. I like helpin' people."

He led them in silence down the road to the house where the Badlows lived. He felt relieved by the news that it was the Badlow twins who had bought the bath chair and its occupant. Though of great physical strength and wickedness for their age, the twins were only four years old. It ought to be quite easy to force them to surrender their purchase and to invent some explanation for its disappearance from the wood. The Badlow twins might easily have mistaken the old man for their grandfather, to whom the old man probably bore a striking likeness, and, finding him in the wood, had been inspired by filial devotion to bring him home. They had probably only just realised their mistake. William's spirits rose as he walked round to the back of the Badlows' house. But they sank when he saw

95

the bath chair standing in the back yard without its occupant.

He uttered his whistle and the twins' elder brother, a harassed-looking boy of William's age, but of exemplary character, appeared at the side door. Owing to his exemplary character, he was not a very intimate friend of William, but there was no actual hostility between them.

William pointed to the tenantless bath chair.

"Where is he?" he gasped.

"Who?" said the brother.

"The man that was in that."

"That? The twins have been playing with that. They've been using it for a tunnel for their train."

"Y-yes, but where's the man that was in it?"

The twins' brother looked at the chair without much interest.

"Was there a man in it?" he said.

"Yes," stammered William. The whole thing was beginning to assume the proportions of a nightmare. "There was a man in it asleep."

"P-raps he woke up an' got out."

"No," said William, "he couldn't have done. He'd got a sort of sleeping disease. He can't wake up. Not possibly he can't. We'd tried. Where are they, anyway?"

"The twins?"

"Yes."

"Mother's taken them into Hadley to get some new shoes."

"When will they be back?"

"Not till bed time. They're going to tea with an aunt when they've got their shoes."

"Crumbs!" said William desperately.

"What's the matter?"

"Din'—din' they say *anything* about an ole man?"

"Wait a minute," said the twins' brother slowly. "Yes, they did, too. I remember now one of 'em said, 'Narsy ole man in it. Din' want him. Frew 'im away.'

I remember now. John said that. He said: 'Narsy ole man in it. Din' want him. Frew him away.' "

"*Golly!*" gasped William. "Did he say where he'd thrown him away?"

"No. He just said that. I didn't take much notice when he said it, but now I remember. He said that."

"An' he din't say any more than that?"

"No."

"An' they won't be back till bed time?"

"No."

"Crumbs. It's one of the awfullest things that's ever happened to me, losing an ole man like this. It's all Victor's fault for selling him to them."

"What is?" said the twins' brother innocently.

But William was walking slowly back to his friends.

"Well?" they said anxiously.

"I—I'm afraid that it was a mistake," said William faintly. "I—I'm afraid that it was this boy's brother an' that they only *thought* they saw a man in a bath chair, but they weren't sure."

"Anyway," said the girl, "it mightn't have been the same man."

"No," said William, brightening, "I don't think it was."

"And, anyway," said the young man, "thanks awfully for trying to help us."

William held out a hand for the half-crown and pocketed it gratefully.

Just opposite the Badlows' gate where they were standing was the entrance to a farm and the farmer was just now coming down the road to it. Like most farmers of the district he cherished no great love for William and his band.

He glanced coldly and suspiciously at William, then turned beaming expansively upon his companions.

"G'd afternoon, Mr. Charles," he said, "how's the major?"

"He's—he's——" began the unhappy Charles and

97

ended abruptly. "You haven't seen him this afternoon
by any chance, have you?"

"No, but he was looking fine last time I seed him.
I were just thinkin' of you, Mr. Charles," he went on.
"I want to show you my Henrietta. You remember
me showin' you her when she was a little one. Her's
fine, now. You did ought to see her. Her's just in
here."

He swept them all into his farmyard. He didn't
actually invite William. In fact, the look he cast on
William was the reverse of inviting. But William
could not resist the temptation entering the farmyard
thus under the shield of an invitation that might be
supposed to include himself, nor could he endure to
leave the adventure in this incomplete state.

The first sight that met their eyes was that of
Henrietta fraternising with some hens and a goat in
the middle of the farmyard. Henrietta was a pig of
enormous proportions. The farmer looked at her in
surprise.

"Well, I'll be blessed," he said, scratching his head,
"how the blazes did she get out? I left her in her
sty."

He opened an immaculate pigsty and invited
Henrietta into it. Henrietta entered. They all leant
over the low wall—the farmer, the young man, the
girl, and William—while the farmer pointed out the
excellences of Henrietta to them with his stick.
Henrietta, becoming suddenly shy, disappeared into
her sleeping quarters.

"Her's as fine a hannimal," pronounced the farmer
as she departed, "as you'd find anywheres. You——"
He stopped. Strange sounds were coming from Henrietta's sleeping quarters. They listened in silence,
open-mouthed. The sounds were the sounds of someone slowly awakening and awakening to wrath.

"What the——? Who the——? Where the——?
confound you, sir. What do you mean by it? Where
are your manners, sir? Where were you brought up?

Where were you educated? I say you're drunk, sir, you're drunk. Are you aware, sir, that you're standing on me? *Standing* on me, sir. Get off me, sir, or I'll call the police. You—Good heavens! Where am I? Where am I? Who are you, sir? Good gracious! You're a pig, a pig, sir. Did you know you were a pig, sir? A——"

Slowly, upon his hands and knees, the major emerged before their horrified gaze, followed by the mildly curious Henrietta. Slowly he rose to his feet.

"What," he thundered, "is the meaning of this outrage?"

His question was addressed impartially to the young man, the girl, the farmer, William, and Henrietta.

The young man, feeling that the answer to the question devolved upon him, raised a hand to his brow and said faintly:

"I will leave no stone unturned till I have sifted this matter to the core, sir. You may safely leave it in my hands."

"In your hands?" roared the major. "I left myself in your hands and this is where I find myself. In a pigsty. *A pigsty,* sir. With a pig standing on me. *Standing* on me. A *pig,* sir. *Literally* a pig. How do you account for it? That's what I want to know."

"I—I don't account for it, sir," said the young man still more faintly. "I'm—I'm as mystified as you are."

"Mystified!" bellowed the major. "So you call yourself *mystified,* sir. It takes more than a word like mystified to express my feelings, sir." He then proceeded to express his feelings fairly adequately.

William felt that at this point he should have quietly disappeared. He had seen at once what had happened. The terrible twins had disposed of their encumbrance by the simple expedient of tipping him out of sight into Henrietta's sleeping quarters, releasing Henrietta in the process. But he could not tear himself away. The situation was far too absorbing.

*"What is the meaning of this outrage?" thundered
the Major.*

The major, having adequately expressed his feelings
and having more than adequately expressed his
opinion of the young man, the girl, the farmer, William and Henrietta, remembered suddenly that it was
one of his gouty days, stopped striding to and fro in

"I will leave no stone unturned till I have sifted this matter to the core, sir," said the young man.

the pigsty and began to limp. Then he fastened a terrifying eye upon the farmer.

"Open that gate, sir," he yelled, "and let me out."

The farmer, trembling, opened the door and the major limped out.

"I shall never get over this—never," he bellowed furiously. "Where's my chair? I say, where's my chair? Shock to my system—never get over it. I tell you sir, I feel more like riding in a hearse than a chair."

They had followed him out into the road and there stood his chair. The twins' brother, having surmised that they wanted the chair as well as the occupant, and being a conscientious youth, had kindly brought it across the road and left it for them outside the farm gate.

The young man spoke with unexpected decision.

"I can only repeat, sir," he said, "that I shall not rest till I have sifted this matter to the core."

He turned to look for William. But William had disappeared. There was a determined look in the young man's eye and William had wisely decided to make sure of having spent his half-crown before Fate should compel him to play the part of core to the young man's sifting.

CHAPTER VI

WILLIAM AND THE SNOWMAN

THE Christmas holidays had begun, and, when William and his Outlaws met in the Old Barn to discuss how the four weeks should be spent, it seemed to them that the whole world and the whole of Eternity lay before them.

"If only it'd *snow*," said Ginger. "It's *years* since it snowed. Well, I know for a fact that it's years, because I remember when last it snowed I was quite young. In all the books you read it snows at Christmas, but it never seems to in real life."

"We had a jolly good time last holidays," said Douglas vaguely.

"We'd got Brent House last holidays," William reminded him mournfully.

Their last holidays had consisted of a glorious possession of an empty house and garden. The agent in whose hands it was lived in the next town, and never visited it, and people in general didn't seem to care whether the Outlaws took possession of it or not. Indeed people in general seemed to prefer that the Outlaws should take possession of it. People's attitude in general appeared to be that if the Outlaws were there they could not be anywhere else, which, held the general attitude, was all to the good. So, in the character of pirates, Red Indians, and shipwrecked mariners, the Outlaws played havoc in the garden of Brent House. Their Red Indian camp was pitched on the rose bed, and whatever fruit they found in the kitchen garden they consumed in their characters of shipwrecked mariners, or cannibal chiefs. The trees were ships in which as pirates the Outlaws attacked each other with all the ruthlessness of internecine warfare. They found their way into the house without much difficulty, and there devised a new game, in which a gang of criminals (Ginger and William) and a gang of Scotland Yard men (Douglas and Henry) pursued each other furiously up and down stairs and held deadly hand-to-hand struggles wherever they happened to meet.

One particularly ferocious struggle took place on the landing and the four of them, still fighting wildly, rolled down the stairs in a confused heap. It was during this episode that one of the bannisters got broken. None of them could account for the breaking of the landing window, though they remembered quite plainly that it was when the house was a fortress in which William was beseiged by a hostile army of Douglas and Henry, and Ginger, as the relieving force, had thrown apples up to him, that most of the bedroom windows got broken.

Even the Outlaws, who looked at their misdeeds through the rosiest of rose-coloured spectacles, realised that their tenancy had not actually improved the property, though they had taken possession of it with the firmest intentions of preserving what newspapers call its amenities. In fact William had said that their occupation of it was a kindness to its owner.

"We can't possibly do it any harm," he had said, "an' we'll keep it aired for him with breathin' in it."

It wasn't till they heard that the property was sold that they stood back, as it were, and surveyed their

103

handiwork. The result was depressing. Even William, that hardy optimist, felt apprehensive qualms.

"Crumbs!" he said. "I didn't know—I say, who broke the greenhouse roof like that?"

"You did," said Ginger, "falling out of the pear tree."

"I bet I never did! Well, p'raps I did. Any way it was you that dug that hole in the lawn."

"Well, I was lookin' for hidden treasure. And it was you that broke the top off the sundial."

"Well, I was tryin' to find how it worked. And there aren't any works in it so it must've been broke anyway. An' it was you that broke the garden seat tryin' to make a boat out of it."

But they realised that they were all equally involved and that the best thing was to hasten from the scene as quickly as possible before any responsible person came to examine the property.

They went to a spot at the other end of the village, and played the mildest games they could think of for a whole day (they even descended to Blind Man's Buff, in the hope of persuading people that they had been playing those games on that spot all the holidays.

Rumours reached them about the new occupants of their paradise. The owner was elderly and extremely irritable, and his niece, who was to keep house for him, was young and extremely beautiful. It was Robert who unwittingly told William that the niece was young and extremely beautiful. Robert's latest "affair" had been terminated by the removal of the goddess and her family from the neighbourhood, and to Robert life without a goddess was simply not worth living. After one glance at the newcomer he had decided that she was worthy to be raised to the unoccupied pedestal, and so ingenuous was he that within five minutes of the decision the whole family knew of it.

"Sickening!" muttered William fiercely to his Outlaws. "Well, all I hope is that if ever I begin to go red whenever anyone says a girl's name someone'll stick a knife in me."

"I will," promised Ginger obligingly.

William had, of course, ample reason for disliking this new affair of Robert's. He wanted as little friendship between his family and the new tenant of Brent House as possible. He had heard that the new tenant was most indignant at the state in which he had found his property. He was reported to have said that the whole Zoo might have been let loose on it. After searching inquiries in the neighbourhood, however, he had narrowed down the "whole Zoo" to the Outlaws with William as their head, and he had promptly gone to see William's father to insist that justice should be done on William. William's father, with what William considered unnecessary officiousness, listened sympathetically to him, and did justice on William. William persisted that Robert had betrayed him to the goddess, who in her turn had betrayed him to her uncle, who in his turn had betrayed him to his father. Robert said scornfully that he didn't take enough interest in his silly affairs to talk about them to anyone, but he was glad that he'd got his deserts for once, and as far as he was concerned he only wished he'd got twice as much.

Robert had reasons of his own for feeling bitter. His affair with the new goddess was not running smoothly. Colonel Fortescue, the uncle, was putting every possible obstacle in its way, and for that Robert in his turn, blamed William.

"I don't blame him," he said, meaning the Colonel not William. "I'd feel the same if I was in his place. I'd feel I'd rather be put to death by torture than have anyone that belonged to me marrying into a family that had William in it. I can hardly count the number of times that boy's utterly messed up my life."

The goddess—whose name was Eleanor—opposed this view, though not from friendliness to William.

"I know he's simply awful," she said, "but it's not

105

because of him that uncle doesn't want me to have anything to do with you. He's always the same who-ever it is. Except Archie. It's because of Archie that he doesn't want me to have anything to do with any-one else."

Archie, it appeared, was the only son of an old friend of her uncle's who had once saved his life. Her uncle, despite his unromantic appearance, cherished romantic views, and thought that your only niece ought always to marry the only son of your old friend who has saved your life. Archie seconded this attitude, and the niece was maddeningly dutiful.

"It isn't that I like him better than you," she said to Robert. "I don't . . . I don't really. But uncle's always been so good to me and I like to please him."

When Robert, who always took a dramatic view of a situation, asked her if she really wanted to blast his whole life, she assured him that she didn't, but she had to *pretend* to be nice to Archie because it would hurt Uncle's feelings if she didn't.

Then Archie appeared on the scene and he turned out to be as handsome as a maiden's dream, though Eleanor assured Robert quite fervently he wasn't hers.

Robert made praiseworthy efforts to win his way into the Colonel's good graces. Eleanor had told him that the Colonel was interested in Roman Britain, so Robert bought a book on Roman Britain and sat up far into the night, with a damp towel round his head, studying it. But he never got a chance of using it. The Colonel glared at him whenever they met with such ferocity that Robert's smile of greeting froze on his lips, and his views on Hadrian's Wall never got a chance of airing themselves. Even Eleanor passed him by without recognition when she was with the Colonel.

"I simply daren't, Robert," she explained. "Ever since he knew you'd asked me to go to a dance with you he's been furious. I simply daren't look at you. He's always like this with men because of Archie."

Robert, of course, persisted in laying all this at
106

William's door, but William had troubles of his own and wasn't interested in Robert's.

When Colonel Fortescue and his niece were firmly and finally in possession of their property, the Outlaws discovered that they had left in it a telescope that one of Ginger's uncles had given him and that was their dearest treasure. All its vital organs were missing, but it was still—in appearance at any rate—indubitably a telescope, and the Outlaws would cheerfully have consigned all their other property to the flames rather than lose it. They held many anxious meetings to discuss their plan of action, and it was with feelings of conscious virtue that they finally decided to walk boldly and honestly up to the front door of Brent House and request the return of their treasure. They agreed to take an equal chance in this adventure by presenting themselves at the front door in a row, so that none should have any advantage by being at the back or disadvantage by being at the front.

It happened that the front doorstep was so narrow as only to accommodate two people with any comfort, and so this arrangement was more difficult than they had imagined. However, the Outlaws were not in the habit of abandoning a plan merely because it turned out to be difficult of accomplishment, and so when the housemaid opened the door she found four boys standing sideways on the narrow doorstep, holding on to each other in order to keep their positions.

"Please can we speak to Colonel Fortescue?" said William. He tried to turn his head to address her, but was wedged so tightly in between Ginger and Henry that all he could address was the back of Ginger's collar.

The housemaid stared at them for some minutes in amazement, then disappeared. She returned almost immediately.

"He says what do you want?" she said, still gazing at them open-eyed and open-mouthed.

"Please, we very kindly want our telescope," said

107

William politely, still addressing the back of Ginger's collar. "It's in the summer-house."

The maid disappeared again but soon returned.

"He says you'd better try goin' to the summer-house the way you went before he came here," she said.

Then she shut the door firmly yet reluctantly, as if she could hardly bear to lose sight of these strange tightly-packed figures.

William stepped down, and the four of them drew a much-needed breath.

"Crumbs!" said Ginger, "I think I'd almost rather go alone to see him than stand packed up like that."

"Well, what did he mean?" said Douglas.

They had hastened out of the enemy's territory, and stood in a little group at the front gate.

"I think he meant that we could go'n' fetch it," said William. "I think that he was giving us permission to go'n' fetch it."

The others were not so sure of this, but William's optimism was proof against all their doubts.

"I'm cert'n that he meant he was givin' us permission to get it," said William. "I think he's feelin' sorry he made such a fuss to my father. I'm goin' in to get it anyway."

So William crawled through the hole in the hedge that had once been a small one but that their summer's occupation had worn to ample proportions, and, entering the lost paradise, strode boldly up to the summer-house, watched from the road by his faithful band. And then from behind the summer-house stepped out Colonel Fortescue. With a roar of fury he seized William, and, in the presence of his horror-stricken followers, executed severe corporal punishment upon his protesting and wriggling person.

William's first thought after this outrage was to put its retribution into higher hands. He thought that his father would be able to avenge it more adequately than he could.

"He'll go to the police about it," he explained to

the Outlaws, "and they'll listen to him, 'cause he's grown up. They never listen to me. I've often tried goin' to them about things. I bet my father'll get him put in prison for life."

But William's father's attitude was disappointing. He merely said that he would thank Colonel Fortescue personally the next time he met him, and expressed the wish that other householders in the district would deal with William in the same way instead of bothering him with complaints.

"Yes," said William bitterly, "it's just like him. Some fathers would wipe out an insult like that with blood. I only hope," he added darkly, "that he won't live to be sorry."

It was in such moments as this that William summoned a picture of the future in which he was a world-potentate, and his father knelt before him and begged for his life. This picture restored his self-respect, and he assumed his most sinister world-potentate manner as he continued:

"Yes, I shun't be surprised if he lives to wish he'd done something a bit different when his only son was insulted with a deadly insult what ought to be wiped out with blood. At least," he added, remembering facts, "one of his only sons, which is just the same."

That, of course, reminded him of Robert, so he went to Robert, and pointed out to him the duty of a brother whose only brother is brutally assaulted.

"You can go an' treat him the same as he treated me," he said, "or you can get him put into prison. I don't mind which. But someone's gotter do *something* about a deadly insult like that. It oughter be wiped out with blood."

But Robert's answer was merely a bitter laugh, and an ironical admonition to William to try if he couldn't mess up his life a bit more.

"Likely he'll let me *look* at her now, isn't it?" he said, "thanks to you and your monkey tricks."

William decided to keep Robert in suspense even

longer than his father, when he was a world-potentate and Robert came to plead for his life.

The situation had been intensified by Archie's coming to spend Christmas at Brent House. The sight of Archie walking past the house with Colonel Fortescue and the beautiful Eleanor raised Robert's resentment against Fate in general and William in particular to fever pitch.

"If I'd had anyone but you for a brother," he said, "I might have won her by now."

"And if I'd had anyone but you for a brother," retorted William as bitterly, "I wouldn't be goin' about with an insult what ought to be wiped out with blood still unavenged."

So affairs stood when the Christmas holidays began, and hence the mournfulness with which William said:

"We'd got Brent House last holidays."

It was the double mournfulness of a paradise lost and a deadly insult unavenged.

"Never mind," said Ginger, trying to lighten the general gloom of the atmosphere, "I'll bet it'll snow. I bet you anything that we wake up to-morrow and find it snowing."

"And I bet you anything we don't," said William, refusing to have the general gloom lightened.

But Ginger was right. They woke up the next morning to find the ground thickly covered with snow. Even William's determined mournfulness wasn't proof against that. Moreover, Robert lost his voice and developed what he called a "funny feeling," and Mrs. Brown, finding that his temperature was 101°, put him to bed and sent for the doctor.

William tried not to feel elated by this, but he couldn't help feeling that it was a judgment on Robert for refusing to avenge him, and so it was with the blithe spirit of one who sees the guilty stricken down by a just Providence that William set out to spend the afternoon with the Outlaws.

The afternoon passed quite pleasantly. After an exhilarating snowball fight which degenerated into an indiscriminate stuffing of snow down necks, and in which they all became soaked to the skin, they decided to make a snowman.

They worked hard for an hour and the result was, they considered, eminently satisfactory. The snowman was life-size, and well proportioned, and his features, marked out by small stones by William, denoted, the Outlaws considered, a striking and sinister intelligence. Having made him, they considered next what to do with him.

"Let's pretend he's a famous criminal an' have a trial of him," suggested William.

The others eagerly agreed.

William was to be the judge, Ginger counsel for the prosecution, Douglas counsel for the defence, and Henry the policeman.

They stood in a row facing him, and William addressed him in his best oratorical manner.

"You're had up for being a famous criminal," he said sternly, "and you'd better be jolly careful what you say or you'll get hung."

The snowman evidently accepted the advice, and preserved a discreet silence.

"The policeman says," went on the judge, "that you've murdered forty people an' stolen over a hundred jewels an' that he had an awful job in catching you. You oughter be ashamed of yourself, carryin' on like that. This gentleman," pointing to Ginger, "is goin' to make a speech against you, an' this gentleman," pointing to Douglas, "is goin' to make a speech for you, an' if I think you did it you're jolly well goin' to get hung."

Ginger stepped forward to address the prisoner.

"Ladies an' gentlemen," he began, then stopped and looked at the prisoner with distaste. "Couldn't we get a coat an' hat for him? He looks so silly like that. He doesn't *look* like a crim'nal. You can't imagine him

111

goin' into shops an' places an' stealin' things all naked like that."

William accepted the suggestion with enthusiasm.

"Yes," he said, "it's a jolly fine idea. . . . *Tell* you what!" he added excitedly, "I'll get Robert's coat an' hat. He's in bed with a sore throat, an' he won't know, an' anyway it's not wrong, 'cause he can't use them so someone else might as well. I'll go'n' get 'em now."

Fortunately, no one was in the hall, and he had no difficulty in abstracting Robert's hat and coat from their peg on the hat-stand. The coat was a new coat of a particularly violent check that Robert's friends rather regretted, and that Robert had bought in a desperate moment when he felt that he must do something to cut out the wretched Archie or die. Certainly when wearing the coat he was such a striking figure that anyone would have looked at him first whoever he was with, but that was all that could be said for it. The goddess's attitude to it was polite but reserved, and even Robert himself was beginning to feel a little doubtful about it. William, however, had no doubts about it at all, and draped it round the shoulders of his snowman with feelings of deep gratification. The hat he tilted slightly forward at a sinister angle over the stone eyes.

"Well," he said, with a sigh of satisfaction, "I bet he looks as much like a crim'nal as anyone *could* look. Now go on, Ginger."

Ginger again stepped forward and began his speech.

"Ladies an' gentlemen. . . . What I've gotter say is that this man's a crim'nal, an' if anyone says he isn't I'll smack their heads for them. I watched him goin' into a jeweller's shop, an' stealin' a hundred pearl necklaces, rare an' valuable pearl necklaces, worth at least a pound each." He addressed the prisoner "Did I or didn't I see you go into the shop an' steal a hundred rare an' valuable pearl necklaces, worth at least a pound each?" The prisoner continued silent.

"You see," said Ginger triumphantly, "he can't say I didn't. . . . An' I've seen him killin' folks too. Hundreds of 'em. Shootin' 'em an' such-like. He's a murderer as well as a robber. Well"—he addressed the prisoner again—"haven't I seen you murderin' folks?" The prisoner still preserved silence. "There!" said Ginger triumphantly, "he can't say I haven't. Well, I've proved he's a murderer an' a robber an' "—to Douglas—"I don't jolly well see how you can unprove it."

"Well, I jolly well do," said Douglas. "If you saw him taking valuable pearl necklaces, why didn't you stop him? An' if you saw him shootin' folk, why din' you stop him? I don't b'lieve he did it at all. I b'lieve it was you what did it an' you're tryin' to put it on to him." He addressed the snowman. "Can you honestly say that it wasn't this man that did it?" The snowman still maintained silence. "There!" said Douglas triumphantly. "He can't honestly say it wasn't you that did it, so it *was* you that did it."

"If he didn't do it," said Ginger, "let him say he didn't do it."

"He daren't," said Douglas, " 'cause you've told him that if he tells on you you'll cut his throat, but I can tell by the way he's lookin' at me that he didn't do it. He's tellin' me as plain as possible by the way he's lookin' at me that he din' do it an' you did."

"Oh, is he?" said Ginger. "I'll tell you what he's sayin' by the way he's lookin' at you. He's sayin'——"

But at this point William interrupted them with an excited exclamation of "Look!"

They looked at the path that led through the field, and there was Colonel Fortescue coming along slowly, his eyes on the ground. It was quite obvious that he had not seen them.

"Quick!" whispered William, retreating into the shelter of the wood that bordered the field. "Quick! Make snowballs for all you're worth."

113

He felt that at last Fate had delivered his enemy into his hands. The Outlaws worked with a will, and, by the time Colonel Fortescue had come abreast with them, they had a good store of ammunition.

"One, two, three—go!" whispered William.

The startled Colonel suddenly received—from nowhere, as it seemed to him—a small hail of snowballs. They fell on his eyes and ears, they filled his mouth, they trickled down his neck. He was blinded, deafened, winded by them. But not for long. The frenzy of the attack abated, and, as his sight and wind returned to him, he looked round furiously for the author of the outrage. Dusk was falling, but he plainly saw a figure in a coat and hat standing at the end of the field near the wood. No one else was in sight.

The snowballs had come from that direction. There wasn't the slightest doubt in the Colonel's mind that the figure in the coat and hat had thrown them. He strode across to it, trembling with rage. His rage increased as he approached. The Colonel was short-sighted, but he knew that coat. It had dogged him and haunted him in his walks with Archie and his niece. It clothed the form of the presumptuous youth who dared to try to thwart his plans for his Eleanor's happiness.

By the time he reached it his rage had passed the bounds of his self-control.

"You impudent young puppy!" he said. "How dare you . . ."

Words failed him. He raised his arm and struck out with all his might.

Now a thaw had set in soon after the Outlaws had finished the snowman, and Robert's tweed coat—which was very thick and very warm—had completed the effect. As the Colonel struck the figure, it crumpled up, and lay, an inert mass, at his feet. He gazed down at it through the dusk with eyes that

114

started out of his head with horror, then with a low moan turned and fled from the scene of his crime.

The Outlaws crept out from behind the bush that had concealed them. William's feelings were divided between elation and apprehension.

"Crumbs, we got him all right!" he said. "I got one in his eye an' one in his ear an' two down his neck. Crumbs, wasn't it funny when he knocked the snowman down! . . . But, I say, I'd better be gettin' Robert's hat an' coat back. Ole Colonel Fortescue'll be tellin' someone an' gettin' me into a row. . . . Let's take the snowman into the wood, too, then we can pretend we never had one here if anyone makes a fuss about Robert's coat."

They bundled up Robert's hat and coat, and rolled what was left of the snowman into the wood. Before they could make their escape, however, they saw the form of Colonel Fortescue, returning through the dusk, and hastily took shelter again behind the bushes. The gallant Colonel was not alone. Archie was with him. They both looked pale and frightened. When they reached the spot where the snowman had been, they stopped, and the Colonel looked about him on the ground, his eyes and mouth wide open with terror. Then he took out a handkerchief, and mopped his brow.

"Great heavens!" he said, "it's gone."

"What's gone?" said Archie.

"The corpse. I left it just here."

"It couldn't have gone. You couldn't have killed him."

"I did, Archie, I swear I did. I shall feel it to my dying day. He crumpled up and fell like a log. Like a log. I must have hit some vital organ. I've never killed a man before, but there was no mistaking it. It was a dead man that fell." He took out his handkerchief and mopped his brow again. "Good heavens, what shall I do?"

"You say he'd been snowballing you?"

"Yes. He'd thrown about a dozen in quick succession. I lost my temper, Archie. I'd got snow in my mouth and eyes and ears and down my neck. I went up to him, and hit out with all my strength. I must be a stronger man than I thought. He went down at my feet like a log, and lay there without a movement, and, if ever a man was dead, he was. Archie, it's the most horrible thing that ever happened to anyone. I—I don't know what to do. I merely meant to teach him a lesson. I didn't want to kill him."

"What on earth was the fellow snowballing you for?"

"Looking back on it, Archie, I think that he must have been suffering from temporary insanity. I'm short-sighted, as you know, but I did notice just before I struck the fatal blow that he looked very pale. Pale and wild-looking. I'm afraid that the poor fellow must have been out of his mind. It's—horrible to think that I killed him. I wonder—Archie, do you think a jury would consider it done in self-defence? I mean, would his snowballing count an assault?"

"You're sure it was young Brown?"

"Absolutely. I recognised his coat even before I saw his face."

"You couldn't have killed him, Uncle, or his body would have been here."

"He fell without a cry or a moan, and lay there like a log. I shall remember it to my dying day. And my dying day, Archie, may be nearer than I think!"

"But still he's not here now. He may have——"

"Crawled into the woods to die," supplied the Colonel wildly, "or crawled home. . . . If he got anywhere in time he'd tell them . . . Archie, the police may be out looking for me now. I came straight back to you, Archie, because I knew I could depend on you. I knew you'd stick by me through thick and thin."

But Archie seemed to have views of his own on that subject.

"That's all very well, Uncle," he said. "I'm—I'm

frightfully sorry for you and all that, but—well, but you can't expect me to mix myself up in an affair of this sort. You've got yourself into this mess, and I'm afraid you'll have to get yourself out of it as best you can."

"You mean you won't stand by me, Archie?" said the Colonel pathetically. "Think of—Eleanor!"

"If you're going to be tried for murder, I'm afraid that it's not much use my standing by you. Honestly, Uncle, I've got my reputation to think of. No man can afford to be mixed up in a case of this sort. Besides"—his voice rose to a frightened squeak—"how do I know that I mayn't be brought into it too? You shouldn't have brought me here, Uncle. People may say that I did it. . . ."

"What are you going to do then, Archie?"

"I'm sorry, Uncle, but I'm going straight back to pack my things, and I'm going home to-night. I'm sorry not to be able to stay over Christmas, after all, but, if things are as you say, you won't be wanting visitors. You may not even be at home to entertain them."

And the gallant Archie turned, and scuttled away through the snow to pack his things.

The Colonel turned and staggered brokenly away towards the Browns' house.

William, however, had got there first. William had run home by a short cut, hung up Robert's hat and coat on the hat-stand, and slipped upstairs to Robert's bedroom to see how he was. Robert was asleep, but his mother, much touched by the proof of William's brotherly solicitude, said that the doctor had been and left him some medicine.

"I'll tell him as soon as he wakes up that you came to see how he was," she said. "He can't talk yet, of course."

William slipped downstairs and waited at the front gate till Colonel Fortescue arrived. The Colonel stopped at the gate, looked irresolutely at the front door, then took out his handkerchief and mopped his brow.

"Robert's very very ill," volunteered William.

Colonel Fortescue gave a gasp.

"He's—he's got home?" he said.

"Oh yes," said William.

"Did he—did he crawl home?"

"I don't know," said William. "I didn't see him come home."

"Have—have they had the doctor?" gasped the unhappy Colonel.

"Oh yes," said William, "they've had the doctor."

"And—and does he think he'll live?"

"Yes," William reassured him, "he seems to think he'll live all right."

"Er—what has he told the doctor about—about what happened to him?"

"He can't speak yet," said William.

"He's unconscious?"

"Yes," said William. "I've jus' been up to his room an' he's quite unconscious."

"But you're sure they think he'll live?"

"Oh yes. They think he'll live," William reassured him.

The Colonel heaved a sigh of relief and mopped his brow again.

"It's a great relief to know that. I—I'll go home now. I'm in no fit state to interview your father or anyone just at present. I'll come round again in the morning and perhaps you'll be about to let me know how he is."

He walked on slowly down the road, and William turned three cartwheels in the middle of the road. He was enjoying his little revenge.

The next morning it happened that Robert received a letter from a friend who had been at college with him last term, but had now left to take up the study of law. He wrote to say that he was passing through the village on his motor-cycle, and would call to see

"Does the doctor think he'll live?" asked the Colonel.

Robert. Robert was much better that morning, and
his voice had partly returned, so the doctor said that
he might see his friend for a few minutes. The friend
was with him when the Colonel arrived to find William
awaiting him by the front gate. The Colonel looked
as if he had passed a sleepless night.

"Well!" he whispered hoarsely, "how is he?"

"He's just a bit better this morning," said William.

119

"Thank Heaven!" gasped the Colonel.

"He can talk a bit this morning," said William, "he's got a lawyer up in his bedroom now."

"A lawyer!" gasped the Colonel. "He's—he's going to summon me for assault, I suppose?"

"I dunno," said William. "They're talkin' about somethin' but I dunno what."

"Better than a summons for murder," muttered the Colonel, "but terrible—terrible all the same. . . . Your father isn't in, is he?"

"No," said William, "he's gone to work."

"Yes—well, it's better perhaps to let things take their course. An apology in such a case is almost an insult. . . . I'll come round again to-morrow and you must tell me how he is."

The doctor was just coming out of the gate the next morning when the Colonel reached it. The Colonel averted his head so as not to catch the doctor's eye, and the doctor made a mental note that the old boy looked a bit queer. The old boy, in fact, looked so haggard that William—who liked to temper justice with mercy even in the case of his enemies—decided to give him a little reassurance.

"The doctor's been an' he's a lot better to-day," he said reassuringly.

"I'm glad," said the Colonel, "devoutly glad. And—and now they know the whole story from him what steps are they going to take about it?"

"They don't know anything from him," said William.

"What?" gasped the Colonel, "hasn't he told them anything?"

"No," said William, "he's not told them anything."

"You mean—they think he was just suddenly taken ill?"

"Yes," said William, "they think he was just suddenly taken ill."

"Noble fellow!" said the Colonel, evidently very

120

much relieved. "Noble fellow! How—how different from that viper I've been cherishing in my bosom."

"You gotter viper?" said William with interest.

"Not now," said the Colonel, "I've cast him out."

"You shouldn't have done that," said William regretfully. "They're jolly rare things an' someone else might've liked it. . . . Anyway the doctor says he can come out for a little walk to-morrow if it's fine."

"Well, my boy, if you'll let me know what time he's coming out, I'd be most grateful to you. And—and I'm sorry for what happened the other day, my boy. You may come and play in my garden any time you like."

He walked slowly down the road, and William turned four cartwheels to celebrate the final wiping out of the insult. But the situation was a complicated one, and it seemed as if the meeting between the Colonel and Robert would complicate it still further. William, however, could not resist being present at this meeting, though he was poised on one foot, ready to turn and flee the minute the finger of guilt pointed in his direction.

Robert had spent the period of his retirement from the world brooding over the far from smooth course of true love, till the Colonel appeared to him to be a veritable monster of cruelty. It was a surprise, therefore, on emerging from the house for his first walk, well muffled and wearing the famous tweed coat, to find the Colonel waiting for him at the garden gate. His surprise increased when the Colonel seized his hand and said brokenly:

"Forgive me, my boy, forgive me."

Robert was deeply touched by the sudden repentance on the part of his enemy.

"It's quite all right, sir," he said. "Don't speak of it."

"I—I've done you a terrible wrong, my boy," went on the Colonel.

Robert, remembering the snubs he had suffered at

the Colonel's hands, quite agreed with him, but was ready to be generous.

"That's quite all right, sir," he said again. "Please don't speak of it."

"I—I'm afraid I hurt you very much indeed," went on the Colonel.

"Well, sir, I can't say you didn't," said Robert, "but—but please don't speak of it."

"You're generous, my boy. Generous. Are you going down the road? Let me accompany you, my boy. Take my arm please."

Robert, rather bewildered by this sudden change of front, took the Colonel's arm, and, making the most of the wholly unexpected situation, said:

"What I've really been wanting to talk to you about, sir, ever since I heard you were interested in it, is Roman Britain. The theory I incline to about the Roman remains at Cirencester . . ." And leapt breathlessly into one of the paragraphs he had learnt by heart from his book on Roman Britain.

The Colonel was enthralled. He completely forgot everything but the Roman remains at Cirencester. In fact, Robert soon began to regret having introduced them. Their possibilities as a subject of conversation seemed so unlimited. He had already repeated the two paragraphs he knew by heart. He had partially learnt a third but he wasn't really sure of it.

They had now reached Brent House, however, and the Colonel called Eleanor out to join them.

"She knows nothing," whispered the Colonel in a conspiratorial fashion as she came out, "don't speak of it to her."

"No, sir, I won't," said Robert, thinking that the Colonel was referring to the Roman remains at Cirencester, and, with rising spirits, discussed lighter subjects with her for the rest of the walk.

Mrs. Brown, who was at the gate watching for their return, asked the Colonel and Eleanor to come in to tea. The Colonel's deprecating manner rather bewildered her, but she was glad to see him being so very friendly (almost affectionate) with Robert, because she was so tired of hearing Robert tell William that he had ruined his life.

"I'm so glad to find this boy so much better," he said, placing a hand paternally upon Robert's shoulder.

"Yes, he's got over it very well," said Mrs. Brown.

"Better than I feared he would," said the Colonel.

This struck Mrs. Brown as rather an odd thing to say, but, though a queer old man, he was evidently a kind one. Indeed his kindness to Robert was almost overpowering. Mrs. Brown put it down to his having been for a walk with him and so got to know him. Mrs. Brown held a touching belief that it was only necessary to know her children—even William—in order to love them.

William was listening with an amazed relief. He could hardly believe that Robert and the Colonel had actually come back from their walk with the misunderstanding still flourishing merrily between them. He had thought that at the first word one or other would have smelt a rat. He had not to wait long now, however. Already the Colonel was drawing in his breath as if for some momentous speech.

"Mrs. Brown," he said, "I think that the time has come to tell you something that only Robert and I know, and to offer you my heartfelt apologies."

Robert gaped at him. For one delirious moment he thought that the Colonel was going publicly to offer him Eleanor's hand. But the Colonel continued:

"What only Robert and I know, Mrs. Brown, is the cause of his recent severe illness."

"But I do know, Colonel," said Mrs. Brown.

"You do?" said the Colonel, much surprised.

"Yes, his tonsils are too big. I can't think why, because neither mine nor his father's are any size at all to speak of."

"No, Mrs. Brown," said the Colonel. "This noble

boy has deceived you in order to shield me. His tonsils are not too big, or, if they are, it wasn't because his tonsils were too big that he crawled home in such a terrible state the other day. Or, if it was, they were enlarged as the result of a brutal attack by—by one old enough to know better. No, the truth is that on Monday afternoon, foolishly, perhaps, this boy snowballed me, and, very very foolishly, I knocked him down so violently that till I returned with help I thought I had killed him."

He looked round the table. Eleanor and Mrs. Brown were gazing at him with amazement, but their amazement was as nothing to the amazement of Robert. Only William was unmoved, his eyes fixed on the ceiling, his face wearing an expression of seraphic innocence.

"I—I—I—*snowballed* you?" gasped Robert.

"Yes, you young devil!" chuckled the Colonel, relieved to have got his confession off his chest, "and a jolly good shot you are, too. Soaked me to the skin. I can still feel the snow running down my back."

The angelic solemnity of William's face broke up for a second then quickly restored itself.

"I—I—I swear I never snowballed you, sir," gasped Robert faintly.

"Come, come, my boy," said the Colonel. "No need to keep that up any longer. Better let me make a clean breast of it. You never snowballed me? You'll be denying that I knocked you down next!"

"Yes, sir," said Robert still more faintly, "I certainly do."

Robert was pale and earnest. There was no mistaking his sincerity.

"Good heavens!" said the Colonel, "you mean to say you've no memory of it at all? I'm afraid there must have been concussion. I ought to have spoken up sooner. I think"—to Mrs. Brown—"that the doctor must be summoned again. To treat the boy for enlarged tonsils when he was suffering from concussion may be fatal."

But Mrs. Brown, who had been struck dumb with amazement, found her voice at last and assured the Colonel that Robert had been in bed on Monday afternoon. She had been in his bedroom all the time, so she could bear witness to it.

"But, great heavens!" gasped the Colonel. "I saw you as plainly as I see you now. A little pale perhaps, but quite recognisable. Apart from everything else I knew your coat. . . ."

He was assured yet again by both Mrs. Brown and Robert that it could not possibly have been Robert.

"Then it must have been a hallucination!" he said in a voice of awe. "It can have been nothing else than a hallucination. I saw him with my own eyes as plainly as I see him now, dressed in his hat and coat.

" . . . But," the Colonel turned to William, evidently remembering something else, "you said that he was unconscious."

"He was," said William innocently, "he was asleep. I thought that was what you meant."

"You said that his lawyer was with him."

"He was," said William, "his friend's a lawyer."

"You said that——" he tried to remember what else William had said, but failed to remember anything definite. "Well," he said kindly, "evidently our conversation was a series of misunderstandings, with, perhaps, a desire on your part, my boy, to pretend to understand remarks of mine that in the circumstances you couldn't possibly have understood. . . . No, it must have been a hallucination. A hallucination," he repeated, evidently growing reconciled to the phenomenon. "A hallucination sent me by Fate to show me the utter worthlessness of one in whom I had trusted, and to show me the worth and intellect of one whom I had ignorantly despised. I thoroughly enjoyed our talk on the Cirencester remains, my boy, and we must have many others."

He leant over and shook Robert warmly by the hand.

Robert grinned inanely, then turned to meet Eleanor's eyes. They were smiling at him fondly. They told him quite definitely that she really *had* liked him better than Archie all the time. He had to pinch himself to make sure that he was awake. It was all too wonderful to be true. And yet it was jolly mysterious. The old chap had said that he'd seen him as plainly as possible in his hat and coat. In his hat and coat . . . snowballing him. . . . He looked at William. William's face wore a shining look of innocence, his eyes were slightly upraised. Robert knew the look well. . . . That kid had been up to one of his tricks. That he knew something about all this. He'd get hold of that kid to-night, and he'd—— No, on second thoughts, Robert decided not to pursue any investigations that might alter the situation.

He was quite satisfied with the situation as it was.

THE END

Have you read
the other

WILLIAM

*books published
by Armada?*

There is no other boy in fiction quite like William. Richmal Crompton's stories about him have been popular since the 1920's – and he's still a hero of readers today. There are scores more of his hilarious adventures in these Armada books. Have you got them all?

And watch out for more **WILLIAM** books in Armada!